WANTING

Forbidden Obsession Duet 1

LYNN BURKE

WANTING

Gideon is a big bad wolf who doesn't bother with sheep's clothing, an overbearing jackass who hates our combined families as much as I do.

I shouldn't secretly love his possessiveness over me at school.

I certainly shouldn't enjoy the unwanted way my body reacts to him.

My sweet sixteen culminates in the first kiss that I always dreamed of. The nightmare that follows, however, leaves me cold and aching.

I go from wanting…to needing.

But Gideon is gone and I'm about to face the real threat to my innocence.

Alone.

Addilyn

"Addilyn," Mother called from the foyer. Her fake, sugary sweet voice pulled my attention from my cell's screen to make me roll my eyes. "They've arrived!"

"Shit," I muttered while scrambling off my bed, having completely forgotten about our dinner company.

She'd told me to dress when I got home from school, but I'd been too busy scrolling my Chit'n Chat account and catching up with the latest makeup trends while chowing down on Swedish Fish.

A quick glance in my full-length mirror on the back of my bedroom door deepened my frown, but I didn't have time to do as I'd been told three hours ago. I straightened my uniform's plaid skirt and white button-down blouse with its stain from the spaghetti the high school's cafeteria had served for lunch.

"Addilyn!"

Damnit. With how frequently she tossed out punishment, you'd think I'd have learned the lesson of obeying the first time. *I'm so screwed.*

Formal dinner in a too-short skirt and rumpled, stained shirt. Mother's bitch mode would commence in three, two…

The front doorbell gonged as I scurried down the carpeted hallway toward the stairs, counting down to my doom. I paused at the second-floor landing to peek below into the grand foyer, ready to put on a bubbly, dazzling smile that might help with Mother's condescending eye once she caught sight of my attire.

But what waited in the foyer below kept my lips flatlined.

Mother kissed cheeks with a tall man dressed in a suit and yellow tie—her favorite color—the typical type of guy she'd been bringing home for as long as I could remember. Dark hair and clean-shaven, just like my father had been.

But she planned for this one to replace my father for real—she had all but told me the night before.

Lloyd Destil. Newly arrived in Anchorage from sunny California with a handful of…wait for it…*yellow* flowers in a bouquet big enough to please any woman who swooned over such shit.

"Darling," he murmured to Mother, kissing her cheek and whispering something against her ear that turned her cheeks pink.

Gag.

He'd known Mother for all of, what? Two months? Three? The man had no idea what hell awaited him if he decided to stick around.

"They're beautiful," Mother breathed over the flowers, looking up at him through her false eyelashes. "And my favorite color! You remembered."

"I want to be your sunshine like you are mine," Mr. Destil told her with a charming smile.

From my lofty height above him, I rolled my eyes. Mother's newest lover appeared decent enough, I'd give him that. Based on the fine-cut suit he wore, he had money. Broad shoulders and what some girls my age might consider a handsome face.

But there was something about him—

A shiver licked over my skin, goosebumps broke out along my arms, and my head jerked toward the open door beyond the lovey-dovey couple.

The younger Destil that Mother had told me about stepped across the threshold. Seventeen-year-old Gideon. My soon-to-be stepbrother. In and out of juvie, anger issues—I'd heard it all, and being Mother's pure sweetheart, I was told to keep my distance. I was not to allow him to influence me in any way, shape, or form.

And talk about shape *and* form. He was drop. Dead. Gorgeous.

Of course, you are. I huffed from my hiding place while drinking him in. All thoughts of his father vanished as I rubbed at my arms to calm the feverish bumps his appearance had brought on.

Dark hair an unruly mess and a little too long for Mother's tastes topped his tall height. His scruffy jawline was set firm, a frown denting the tanned skin between his eyebrows. He'd dressed for dinner in a suit like his father, but he didn't look pleased about it or the fact he'd been brought north, far away from sunshine and warmth.

Almost an adult though, he wouldn't have to truly deal with a new parent like I would at fifteen.

Lovely. Time to meet the homewreckers.

Not that our home could be any more wrecked.

Telling myself Gideon's good looks didn't matter to me, didn't *bother* me, I lifted my chin and waltzed around the wall I'd hid behind to step onto the landing, feigning confidence as Mother greeted Gideon. I grabbed hold of the railing and forced my hesitant feet downstairs when I usually would've scampered with the smile Mother preferred.

I wasn't dressed to the nines. Hadn't clipped up my curly white-blonde hair or slipped on a pair of high heels like Mother's stilettos. Nothing I did or said at that point would please Mother, so why try?

Three pairs of eyes staring at me caused my stomach to clench up tight.

Mother handed over the bouquet to a waiting household staff member, her glare deepening with every downward step I took.

"Lloyd, darling," she purred, linking her arm in his. Her unhappy gaze seared my face as I crossed the foyer toward them. "This is my sweetheart, Addilyn."

I peered up at the man looming beside Mother rather than dealing with her fake-assed smile and the icy orbs that promised I would be hearing her disapproval of my disobedience later.

Mr. Destil's dark-eyed gaze slid down over my school uniform as though sizing me up like Mother did before allowing me out of the house. Unlike Mother's disdain, his eyes held a hint of the smile on his lips.

A shiver of a different sort slid through me, the kind that raises your neck hairs when you're outside in the dark.

"It's a pleasure to finally meet you, young lady." Mr. Destil's low voice rumbled through me.

Tearing my attention off Mother, I stepped back on instinct rather than shake his outstretched hand even though his gaze appeared harmless enough.

"Addilyn," Mother admonished with a tone that let me know I'd be sorry for my bad manners.

"It's quite alright, darling. This is my son,

Gideon," Mr. Destil said rather than making a scene. He turned to motion the younger man forward with the hand I'd refused to shake.

Piercing blue eyes glanced down over the curves I'd inherited from Mother at too young of an age, but rather than feeling weirded out by Gideon's good long look at me, warmth tingled into the tips of my breasts. Heat flooded his eyes when they met mine—but blinked out like a flashlight, his face becoming cold and hard.

And leaving me breathless. Shaky and unsettled in a way I didn't know how to deal with.

"Sis," he said, his tone as mocking as his slow smirk that fluttered my belly.

Proper poise, I could hear Mother's echoing hiss from many times before between my ears.

I lifted my chin to do the same as he'd done to me, my narrowed gaze sliding down over his suit as though I found him lacking in every way—which I totally didn't. Broad shoulders for seventeen, he could have been out felling trees. And that hair… those bedroom eyes, my best friend Jenny would say, could talk a girl into giving up her first kiss.

He stirred things inside me I didn't understand, and I hated him for the curiosity tingling through my limbs and whispering in my mind.

"I'm not your *sis*," I shot back with a huff and flounce of my hair.

"Addilyn Jane!" Mother's sternness tore my gaze

off of him. Lips pressed tight, she told me all I needed to know without a single word of reprimand and consequence.

Bad manners equal loss of privileges, Mother always said, and my only interest since middle school had become my cell phone.

Holding back my sigh, I handed it over, knowing arguing would only keep my cell hidden in her massive walk-in closet for an extra week.

"Well." Her voice brightened, all syrupy sweet again as she tucked the pilfered lifeline away in a pocket of her pale yellow slacks.

So much for calling Jenny later and filling her in on the latest shit in my life.

"Shall we?" Mother patted Lloyd's arm and led him toward the formal dining room, murmuring about the fish our chef had prepared for dinner as her Jimmy Choos clacked on the marble flooring.

While I was safe for the time being, Mother excelled at hiding her pissiness behind her plastic smile. I'd catch hell for misbehaving later, no doubt.

"I expected you to be a rich little snob, but shit, you give the word new meaning," Gideon said quietly with a sneer, his smirk still fixed in place as he peered down at me.

"Go to hell," I whispered and spun on my heel, following after Mother and Mr. Destil.

"Already headed there, princess," he stated, not loud for enough our parents to hear.

"Don't call me princess!" I growled over my shoulder.

Gideon's gaze plastered to my backside, and those flutters rushed through me again, warming me between the thighs and heating my face.

"Jackass," I muttered, turning around once more, shoulders thrown back.

"Princess."

I wanted to show him exactly how un-princess-like I could be, but hissing like a cat and scratching his eyes out wouldn't go unnoticed or unpunished by Mother.

I sat in my chair instead, a picture-perfect example of a well-bred young woman, even though I wished the floral arrangement Mother had delivered for our dinner hid me from the hot pile of trouble sitting across the table.

Too damn hot for his own good, Gideon could have been a runway model, and I kept stealing peeks whenever Mother engaged him in conversation. Sharp bone structure, full lips that made me dream about sweet sixteen kisses beneath starlit skies. Long eyelashes my friends would die for and that dark hair bordering on inappropriate as Mother would say... My fingers tingled with the need to push it back just so, to fix it with a bit of hair putty. Or perhaps rumple it instead. Even messed up, his hair wouldn't distract from his beauty.

If anything, it added to his appeal.

"So, your mother tells me you're interested in the cosmetics industry."

I whipped my head Mr. Destil's way to find him flashing the charming smile Mother had fallen for.

"Makeup is my passion," I said, glancing at Mother to find her enamored with the man seated beside her. Smiles and stars in her eyes.

"The beautification aspect or artistry for say, Hollywood?"

"It's more a hobby than career interest," I answered with a slight shrug Mother wouldn't approve of. I had no clue what I wanted to do with the rest of my life beyond eventually getting out on my own, away from her, and making independent choices.

Mother mentioned a movie crew that had been in the area the summer before and how Jenny and I had begged to watch them film because of the leading, male actors.

"But they're much too young for such company," she said. "My sweetheart will remain as pure as possible for as long as possible. She hasn't even kissed a boy yet."

I smiled with my teeth even as my face heated and stomach clenched over her prideful tone in telling near strangers personal stuff about me. My *purity* she'd hammered the need for into my brain since childhood was no business of Mr. Destil or his son.

"What a very admirable character, young lady."

"Thank you, sir." I forced myself not to mutter while focusing my attention back on my plate.

The conversation moved on, and I breathed a sigh of relief. At least Gideon kept quiet across from me. He was no smooth-talker or charmer like his father. There was something about him, a sense of danger, darkness almost, that hung over him, but not the kind that suggested I run and hide. A bad boy, perhaps a big bad wolf rather than the rich snob he'd accused me of being.

The perfect cut of his suit marked him as upper class like Mother called us, not that Anchorage had much in the way of rich folk. Father had been the one with money. Mother had been a poor working girl who turned her back on her family to marry up beyond her class.

While drunk once, she'd told me she'd grown up on the bad side of the tracks and would do anything within her power to keep from going back to that life. She never spoke of the family she'd left behind, and when I'd asked about a grandparent last, she looked down her nose and told me they weren't worth our time.

Epitome of a *snob* if ever I'd met one.

But Gideon…

Another quick peek—he watched me with those blue eyes, seeming to assess me with a knowing look. Eyes hooded beneath his tilted back head.

Jackass.

I flashed a prissy smile Mother would be proud of and took a dainty bite of my fish, determined to ignore him.

The girls at school were going to go crazy for that damn half-smile he shot me every time I got caught glaring his way. Jenny would call me a lucky bitch to have him sleeping a shared bathroom's distance away, but I had a bad feeling about the whole idea of two Destil men in our house.

I had hated him and his father long before they'd shown up for our dinner date. Mother had gone to California to sell off a property Dad had owned and returned a changed woman—smiling, with light in her eyes I'd recognized.

She'd met a man.

Instant love.

After a mere week together, she'd agreed to marry him. Wasn't I excited to finally have a father? A brother?

No one would replace the father I barely remembered. And a brother? Someone who would always hit the shared toilet between our bedrooms? Jenny complained nonstop about her two younger brothers, so I expected I had absolutely nothing to look forward to.

No thank you with a capital N, but I knew better than to argue.

Mother had invited them to visit, to move in, but

I shuddered at the thought she unknowingly allowed a couple of vampires into our home. Not that I believed in such things, but still. I could imagine Lloyd biting Mother's neck and sucking her body dry of life's blood.

I could imagine Gideon's mouth on my neck…

I choked on a bite of my risotto. Yeah. Not a good idea at the dinner table.

Scowling at my plate, I squeezed my thighs together.

I could feel Gideon's stare and heat growing where it wasn't supposed to. But I could also sense his father's attention on me from time to time too. At least he didn't make attempts to get me to approve of him like Mother's other boyfriends had done.

I had expected him to prod at me, attempt to manipulate me. Try to read inside my head, see what kind of trouble I might cause in our new wannabe family that would never *be* a family if I could help it.

Mr. Destil actually seemed quite…normal. Unassuming and kind.

A foot bumped against my ankle, and I jerked my head up.

Gideon raised an eyebrow while slowly sliding his shoe across mine.

Eyes narrowing, I pulled my leg back beneath my chair, crossing my ankles and taking another dainty bite of fish as though I couldn't be bothered by his actions.

Did he expect me to react verbally? He obviously had no clue about my mother and all her rules. Boy, was he in for a big surprise.

I couldn't help a quick peek up at him though.

His slow, sexy wink fluttered my belly.

The chef-prepared food turned to cardboard on my tongue. My armpits tingled and grew damp.

I needed to call Jenny later for her advice on how to navigate this new life Mother planned for us, but without my cell, I was lost.

Mother and Mr. Destil chatted about business and his and Gideon's move north—to stay—in a short couple of weeks. His rumbling voice filled my ears with chuckles and the kind of words Mother loved to hear lavished on her.

Beautiful.

Classy.

Sweet and poised.

The perfect woman to have by his side.

Talk about a total gag.

Not huffing became a chore as the hour wore on, and I kept silent since children shouldn't open their mouths at the table unless answering a direct question.

He wants your money, Mother, not your love.

Of course, she didn't hear my thoughts, but she would've waved off my opinion like she always did.

My respect for the only parent I could remember faded more with every passing minute. It had begun when the first gold digger showed up with sweet words and wine. The second, third, and fourth who managed to hold Mother's attention thought manipulating me onto their good sides would help them in their conquests to woo rich Widow Reed.

Sad that even when I was ten I could read their bullshit and Mother couldn't.

Her nagging and their lack of being able to please her in any way—I could empathize with the desperate men on that at least—had each and every one hightailing it out the front door within a matter of weeks.

But Mr. Destil seemed the smart sort, wooing her rather than me with his full of shit one-liners and praise. He knew the words to say like he could hear Mother's needy thoughts that constantly got spilled to me, and his presence at our table, in our home, settled in deep like the hidden reaches of an iceberg beneath darkened water. He wouldn't be going anywhere, anytime soon, I feared. Which meant I *would* be stuck with an older stepbrother. But probably not for long.

Mother's newest man was full of the right things to say, but once he got to know her beneath her fake exterior, he'd take off like all the rest. She'd proven herself unlovable for as long as I could remember.

He would find out who she really was soon enough too.

I dared another peek at the boy I'd be spending time with until that day though.

A very hot stepbrother whose hair fell over his brow while he focused on his food, giving me a moment's reprieve from his unsettling stare.

A jackass who would turn our high school upside down in a few short weeks.

We moved into the parlor after dinner—an honest to goodness sitting room like ancient people had. It was where Mother spent most of her time and I avoided at all costs since I held no memories of fun within its walls—merely instruction and criticism when called into her presence.

Stiff-backed chairs covered in yellow damask didn't appear as welcoming as Mother seemed to think. At least the fireplace's lit logs crackled against the cool, fall air outside the tall windows overlooking the northern mountains. A wall of books. Knickknacks on the tables and mantle. Throw blankets and footstools—all shades of yellow, of course—for getting comfy when Mother wasn't watching close enough to snip at me about proper posture and poise.

Everything sat in its place without a spot of dust thanks to the staff who moved on silent feet and hid in shadows.

They saw everything. Heard every word.

And papers Mother had made them sign kept their mouths shut about what went down in Widow Reed's house.

Mostly the two of us screaming at each other whenever I couldn't keep my mouth shut.

Mr. Destil poured liquor from the decanter of whatever Mother sipped every night and offered her the drink. He went without, I noted. At least her expensive taste in alcohol wasn't what made Mother appealing to him. The last man she'd brought home ended up rip-roaring drunk at our first dinner. That was the last I'd seen of him.

They sat side by side on a couch far from where I had settled near the door, ready to bolt the second she suggested I retire for the night. Mr. Destil angled close to Mother, their knees touching, heads close together while speaking quietly.

Gideon lounged in a chair across from me, and I ignored him, chin lifted, studying the ugly printed paper on the wall above his head as though it held more interest to me than his pretty face.

Stuffy and old fashioned with its golden roses, the wallpaper made my upper lip curl. Mother seriously needed to do some updates—

"Bad enough Dad's gonna drag me all the way up here to Alaska, but to be stuck with a goddamn snob for a sister? Could my life be any more fucked?"

I turned my attention downward, narrowing my gaze and hating that Gideon was close enough to make out a few freckles across his nose. Even more endearing. I prayed he wouldn't reveal dimples if he ever smiled for real. "Pardon me?"

He sprawled in the chair, arms over the back, that damn smirk curling his lips upward. I glanced at Mother, waiting for her to admonish him for his slouching posture, but she couldn't be torn away from her latest lover and whatever bull he spouted against her ear that made her cheeks flush.

"He's weaseled his way in, and now you're stuck with him—and me. Just would be nice if you at least acted—" Gideon glanced down over me with a semi-sneer "—normal so we could get along and shit."

"I *am* normal."

He snorted, his gaze narrowing. "Spoiled, rich princess. You don't know the first thing about a life beyond your mother's money."

As if he did with his expensive clothing, shined shoes, and that rented Mercedes out in the circular drive beyond the parlor's window. Car rental or not, it still cost his father some cash to borrow it for their weekend visit.

While I was only fifteen, I had been through enough heartache to make any person an old soul, not that he knew or cared. I glared harder, hating that my spine stayed straight and my hands clasped lightly in my lap as Mother had taught. "And I suppose you've got it all figured out at the ripe old age of what? Seventeen?" I hissed quietly across the short distance between us.

"Yep." He popped the P and chuckled. "Lived the high life down in sunny, warm California."

"Being sent to a juvenile delinquent center three times in three years and having anger management therapy is hardly the high life," I shot back the gossip I'd heard Mother sharing over her cell with one of her country club friends.

He studied me with those sinful bedroom eyes until I shifted on my seat, but I refused to look away. Mother would have a fit if she heard what I'd said to him.

This boy is going to be major trouble. Major.

He let out a quiet curse but without heat or threat. Gideon's head swiveled his father's way, his brow furrowing same as when he'd first arrived.

My shoulders relaxed at the assurance he wasn't too pleased with what was going on between our parents either. "You hate what they're doing to us too, don't you?" I kept my tone low so Mother wouldn't overhear.

"What gave it away?" That damn smirk—but sarcastic—returned as did his attention full on my face. His eyes held no hint of happiness though.

"It's not *my* fault, you know," I told him, hoping he'd stop taking his anger out on me. "I don't want or need another father."

Gideon raised one eyebrow in a perfect upside-down V like the evil vampire I'd considered him to be. A sexy as hell vampire. One who would nibble on my neck and tell me how good I tasted.

"How about an overly protective stepbrother?" he murmured, his focus sliding down over me.

I crossed my arms over my breasts, trying to hide my nipples' pebbling reaction to his gaze. "And why would you care what I do?"

His gaze lingered long enough on my boobs that my face heated. A slow, genuine smile revealed not one, but *two* dimples, damn him. "Maybe I care more about what those *around* you might do."

2

Gideon

"They may marry, but we'll never be a family," the little princess snipped back rather than acknowledging my little warning. A delicious pink rose on her high cheekbones, her sexy as fuck lips pressing tight as I studied her.

My grin grew, but the truth of the situation I found myself in didn't create one fucking ounce of joy. Dad's latest conquest had a hot as fuck daughter, a few months shy of Alaska's legal age for consent, but when had that stopped him? And the tasty-looking morsel in front of me with the pale legs and gorgeous tits had my mind going the *fuck and conquer* route the second I'd laid eyes on her.

"Dad always wanted a little girl." I gave her the brutally honest truth and waited, wondering how smart Addilyn Reed really was.

She shivered like she caught my drift, and I

glanced over at my dad again where he sat with her mom. His dark eyes lingered on the princess's tits as his soon-to-be wife held his new, ugly as fuck tie, whispering in his ear.

His conquest. *Her* daughter.

Without a doubt, the real reason he'd decided to snag the rich widow as his latest sugar momma. While I hated him for what he did and what he'd done in the past, I hated Addilyn too.

The fish I'd eaten for dinner took to flopping around in my gut like it was fresh off the line, and I swallowed against the bile creeping up my throat. If Mrs. Reed knew Dad's past, she wouldn't have let him step foot into her stately mansion with its marble floor and wrapping stairs. She would have told the bastard to take a hike rather than mess with the fire of my father and the sure tragedy to follow in his wake.

Addilyn slid her hands back onto her lap, her fingers laced together on a plaid skirt that showed too much damn thigh for her own good. A stain on her white button-down, right above her pebbled left nipple drew my focus—again.

With firsthand knowledge of living beneath a controlling parent, I'd seen more than either Mrs. Reed or her daughter had probably expected or meant to show when she'd walked down the stairs like royalty.

Mother Reed didn't appreciate Addilyn's appearance in what had to be a school uniform when she herself wore expensive-looking slacks and a silk blouse of the most hideous vomit-yellow color. Mother Reed's disapproval hurt her daughter deeper than she probably knew too.

Did the blonde beauty with the captivating eyes sitting across from me ever consider rebelling? Had she ever gone against her mother, stretched her wings, said 'fuck you,' and just breathed? She sure as fuck didn't act it—she looked like a sheltered princess, exactly as I'd tagged her.

An innocent one if her reactions to the lust-filled looks I couldn't help giving her when Dad wasn't paying attention were any indication. Sultry mouth parting like she sucked in air. Wide eyes, her pupils dilating the slightest bit. Twice, a flick of her pink tongue to her lower lip.

Those slender fingers of hers tightened together, the knuckles growing whiter the longer I stared, drinking my fill.

She hated me. Hated Dad—rightly so, smart girl. Hated that her mother had brought two strange men into their lives.

Well, I hated her and her pissy attitude too, but what else?

I cocked my head to the side and studied Addilyn Reed, the snobby hot bitch who without a doubt felt me and my dad were way beneath her station even if her mom didn't. Peering down her nose at me even though she was a good ten or so inches shorter definitely came naturally.

Her ankles were crossed, knees pressed tightly together. Prim and proper, shut off except for those few times I got her to hiss and spit like a damn cat. Fucking loved it too. All that pent-up anger I thoroughly understood, the kind that made for one hell of a hot fuck when given the chance. Made me want to poke and prod beneath her exterior. See how far I could get her to go beyond her tight-reined upbringing. See all the shades of red her high cheekbones held beneath her pale skin.

Addilyn had chosen a seat close to the door as though seeking out the quickest way to escape when allowed, but she sat straight, shoulders back, drawing attention to her perfect set of tits.

Her chin was held high and white-blonde hair shone like she brushed it three times a day, but her gaze flitted to my face and away as though my stare caused some deep insecurities to rise inside her. Like I unsettled her—when it should've been Dad alone who sent that shiver down her spine. I'd noticed it when he'd held out his hand to greet her earlier in the foyer.

The twitch of a frown between her perfectly shaped—dark—eyebrows hinted displeasure I'd already figured out and made me wonder what color of hair hid her little clit.

A contradiction, a mystery I wanted to unravel.

And the press of her full lips in continued disdain…

She had lips that would look fucking fantastic glistening with my pre-cum I smeared over them—or wrapped around my dick.

Goddamnit.

My jaw clenched again, and I had to glance away. I hated my tight suit and tie and the stuffy feeling of the parlor as much as Addilyn despised our presence in her house.

No fucking way could I let Dad know what the sight of her did to me. No fucking way could I let him close to her either. I'd been conditioned. Could read a person's body language, their tells—an ability he, thank fuck, didn't seem to possess.

Living with Dad for seventeen, almost eighteen years had taught me well, and I knew what that fucker was after.

Same as before.

Just like with the last ripe peach I hadn't realized he'd wanted or known I'd needed to protect until it was too late.

I'd been in juvie for the third time—for losing my shit after walking in on him with his hand down my stepsister's leggings—when carbon monoxide filled our house. Dad had been out of town on business.

Without a prenup to ensure his dead wife's remaining family inherited her estate, Dad had gotten it all.

A muscle ticked in my jaw as memories battered my head. He hadn't defended himself when I'd given him that black eye, but I'd come to realize what he was capable of. Fear for my own life kept me quiet, and I didn't share my suspicions with the police who'd investigated the little 'accident.'

And in a quiet exchange neither of us spoke about once settled, Dad greased a few pockets to clean up my record.

I hated that I owed him one. But my birthday loomed, and I would find my freedom.

He excused himself to go take a piss—without so many words—and Mrs. Reed watched him walk out the parlor door, a small smile on her lips, eyes shining like a fool in love. Totally smitten with a man she never should've allowed into her bed. She'd been won over by a selfish prick whose bank balance dwindled.

That inheritance from his dead ex-wife? Gambled away.

Almost destitute, he'd found himself a new toy, one with a young daughter, a seemingly virginal young girl ripe for the plucking.

Addilyn didn't even glance his way as he checked out her legs in his periphery while striding past.

The girl definitely had smarts to not be drawn in by my snake of a father—even if she was a bitch.

"You're a very lucky young man to have such a distinguished role model," Mrs. Reed murmured in a breathless tone after Dad shut the parlor's door behind him.

A spew of words filled my mouth, and even though I expected Dad would hear about whatever shit I wanted to say while still fighting off bile at the memories, I didn't give two fucks. I wasn't eighteen, and he couldn't legally toss me out just yet. The fucker was stuck with me until spring.

Besides, the way he looked at Addilyn pissed me the hell off. Fuck him and his bad choices that had left us damn near penniless.

"Lloyd's full of shit," I muttered, lounging back like a sprawled, rebellious teen since I expected the bitch queen wouldn't appreciate it.

Addilyn's head jerked my way, big blue eyes wide as hell, lips parted on a gasp.

"Young man," Mrs. Reed whispered fiercely. "In this household we show respect for our elders!"

I slowly turned my head toward her. My soon-to-be stepmom from hell held her chin high, same as her snobbish daughter. Didn't they realize looking down their noses like that left their necks exposed? Pink spread over Addilyn's mother's cheeks too but not in a way that made me want to keep *her* unsettled. I figured she would expect me to address her Mother like her daughter did, but Mrs. Reed would soon find I did things however the fuck I wanted.

Perhaps I would take to calling her Ingrid, her given name. I expected she would love that shit.

Having zero respect for the widow since she couldn't judge a man's character, I didn't feel the need to show her any. But I knew how to play the game, and the strange, stirring desire to keep her daughter safe for as long as I could restrained my usual rebellion with a tighter than expected leash.

"Yes, ma'am," I murmured, priding myself in keeping the sarcasm from my voice while putting on a full-on smile that always landed me where I wanted. Too bad it hadn't worked on Dad when I learned Ingrid had a daughter and I suggested he find a woman closer to home. And too bad begging to not move to snow country or transfer schools my senior year got ignored.

His newest lover's face smoothed a bit.

Keeping Ingrid happy meant Dad would stay off my back.

Keeping Dad away from Addilyn would keep *me* happy.

Alaska might be cold as fuck without nearly enough sunshine for my liking, and even though I told myself I hated the princess for getting my ass dragged north, she was like a ray of golden sunlight shooting down from the heavens. Feigning disinterest in her sexually and allowing my annoyance loose over having another stepsister would keep us both safe.

I hated her, but I wasn't so much a bastard that I'd allow Dad to get after her ass while I was around.

I would protect her for as long as I could before I hightailed it back to California.

But that didn't mean I couldn't annoy the shit out of her in the meantime. Fuck knew I would need to find something to smile about out in the backwoods of no-man's land for the next couple of months.

3

Addilyn

Mother set me straight on my behavior over breakfast, and I took it without comment, hoping a contrite look and a "yes, ma'am" or two would earn me back my cell phone quicker. Once she finished letting me know how deep her disappointment ran, she settled in with her coffee, glancing at my stooped shoulders.

"Proper poise," she stated, her own chin lifting.

I straightened, wishing I could live up to her high expectations and knowing I never would.

"So, what do you think of him?" she asked before sipping, leaving a half ring of orange-red lipstick on her dainty china teacup.

Honesty or continue with the bullshit, hiding my true thoughts and feelings to keep on her good side?

I hesitated.

"Addilyn. Tell the truth, please." She ordered her

usual command while setting her coffee aside when I didn't answer in a timely fashion.

"I don't like him."

"Why ever not?" She sat straighter if that were even possible, her groomed eyebrows rising. "He's well put together. Has class and impeccable manners. Yes, his son is certainly lacking in many areas, but Lloyd said he's sending him back to California after graduation so his time beneath my roof will be short."

Her roof—not ours. Not the first time I'd made the distinction.

"He gives me the creeps," I continued with the truth as she expected.

"He's seventeen. Harmless."

"I meant the elder one. Lloyd," I muttered, telling myself I ought to just zip my lips and not stir the wasp nest.

"Mr. Destil?"

I nodded, feeling her disappointment keenly, but she *had* asked.

"You said that about the last two men I brought home to meet you." Displeasure pinched her features, her lips, and I knew I'd gone too far—again.

Great. I let out a quiet huff of breath, readying myself for her usual speech about judging people before giving them a chance, calling her lover by his first name, blah, blah, blah.

"You're fifteen, Addilyn Jane," she chided, her

voice like nails on a chalkboard. "Old enough to recognize the fact that I've laid down my life, my desires, to raise the child your father wanted. It's *my* time now," her voice rose, causing me to wince.

Well, shit and good morning to me. The child Father had wanted... Not her.

That was a new one, and it stung. Badly enough that I cringed.

"It's time for me to move on," she continued, ignoring my reaction. "I need to find love again and be happy!"

I stared at my plate, processing. Her words shouldn't have surprised me—everything else was always about her. What made me think our unhappy life of two couldn't possibly get worse?

What made me think she'd care about my opinion enough to listen for a change?

Swallowing, I glanced out the panel of windows overlooking Anchorage in the distance, a city Mother had told me Father once had under his thumb. Doing what, I couldn't be bothered with, since shimmering eyeshadow held my interest more than properties and the stock market.

Father had been one of the very few millionaires in Alaska, killed in a boating accident when I'd been four.

I couldn't remember much more than his smile and that I'd adored sitting atop his shoulders, pretending I was the queen of the world.

But Mother didn't keep any pictures of him around, not that I needed to see them to recognize I didn't look anything like him. A spitting image of my blonde-haired mother with her heart-shaped face, pointed chin, and plump enough lips to never need Botox.

She still had hers done though. Puffed to the point they looked ridiculous, she kept them smeared with an orange-red that did nothing for her pale skin.

But what did I know?

I *did* know—thanks Mother for the brutal honesty—that I had been Father's idea, not hers. I also knew I was only an overly opinionated teenager who loved Chit'n Chat and watched makeup tutorials late into the night.

Well for the next week, I won't.

Turning my focus on my scrambled eggs, I forked up a small bite Mother would approve of, fighting to keep my back straight when all I wanted to do was slouch and let loose the weight pressing against my shoulders. "I hope Mr. Destil makes you happy, Mother," I whispered through the thickness tightening my throat, expecting anything else I attempted to say would end in a catfight. Something I definitely didn't have the energy for.

"Thank you, sweetheart."

Sweetheart. I fought off a huff even as tears burned my eyes.

I put the eggs between my lips and chewed without tasting. Three days before Thanksgiving and I learned my mother hadn't ever wanted a child. That she would marry some stranger thinking he would fulfill her when all I'd ever done was strive for that very thing.

Guess I'd failed one too many times. Hell, I'd failed since the moment of conception.

What a way to start off the long winter ahead of us.

Mother slid my cell across the table, and I glanced up at her, not trusting her offer. "Mr. Destil and I discussed your disobedience last night after you went to bed, and he suggested you must have been caught up in your homework and forgot to change."

Well, holy shit.

I stared—and remembered I ought to nod quickly before she changed her mind.

"Here." She patted my cell. "But next time, please be better prepared for company. We must always put on our best front."

"Yes, ma'am." I tucked my cell into my back pocket, my face muscles tempted to grin.

Mr. Destil had made excuses for me—and he got me my cell back.

Huh.

Mother started in on their wedding plans, and I made noises of approval she would expect while forcing down my breakfast. Once in her good graces, I'd learned it was best to milk it for as long as possible. She would often buy me gifts, probably thinking they would make me forgive her negativity or treatment. Not that she ever apologized for a damn thing.

They would marry after New Year's at the courthouse—because her fiancé didn't want to waste money on a lavish wedding. He just longed to marry the love of his life, the sooner the better.

Gag.

Of course they would take off for a two-week vacation to some islands down in tropical waters, leaving me in the freezing cold in my new stepbrother's care. The good shivers I'd felt upon first seeing him caressed over my skin again.

"And when we return, we'll discuss your birthday party," Mother stated, breathless from her usual excitement over planning get-togethers.

From one party to the next—Mother's favorite pastime outside of the spa.

"Sweet sixteen," she sighed, and I actually smiled, the two of us sharing a cool moment for a change.

Sweet Sixteen. I'd been dreaming of that day for years, ever since I decided boys, Devon Bradshaw especially, weren't so bad after all. I wanted the fantasy of a perfect sweet sixteen more than anything. That first touch from a young man, the brush of his lips over mine.

Or perhaps, I'd heard Mother gush about it for so long that I'd taken on her desires. Hard to tell with an overbearing mother like mine who often complained her parents had never tried to protect her from the world.

"I would love to have a big party here," I dared to suggest, considering our smiles. "Invite all of my friends—not just the girls like we do for slumber parties every year."

Mother's lips pursed as though recognizing my *hint, hint* without the wink.

Aaaand my shoulders slumped.

"I was thinking a nice brunch at the country club. Girls only." She sipped her second cup of coffee. "The last thing I need is for you to end up pregnant as a teenager and have you dumping a kid off on me when you head to college."

Yeah. I'd forgotten for a split second it was her "time to live."

"A brunch would be lovely," I lied, giving her a fake smile she wouldn't bother to check for honesty.

"Pink roses—and I'll buy you a gorgeous vintage gown for the event," Mother continued. "We'll have tea and small cakes…"

So much for waiting until after her honeymoon to plan. Mother went on and on like she always did when it came to parties and making an impression. Showing off her money to the women she called her friends.

More like cackling, gossipy bitches if their monthly brunch at our home told the truth. Fake smiles. Fake boobs. Fake nails. Nothing about them was real except for their money and Mother's love of it.

I tuned her out, wondering what the hell I would do while waiting for the rest of the weekend to end.

"Mr. Destil and his son fly home tomorrow—he has so much to take care of before moving." Off the wall subject change, but whatever. Mother couldn't keep her focus on one thing any more than Jenny's new puppy could.

"So we won't be seeing them today?" Too much hope laced my words, but she didn't seem to catch on.

She glanced down at the gold and diamond-encrusted watch around her wrist. "They should arrive within the hour." A quick look over my attire caused her gaze to narrow. "I would appreciate seeing you wear something a little more...*more*. Mr. Destil is already taken with me, but I want him to be pleased with how I've raised you as well. What you do, how you dress, is a direct reflection of me, Addilyn, and your jeans and that sweater just aren't enough."

How many times had I heard that one?

"Yes, ma'am," I murmured.

"Why don't you run along and get ready, hmm? Leave your hair down and take it easy on the shimmery eyeshadow that makes you look like a whore."

Yeah, thanks for that too, Mother.

Biting my tongue, I considered an afternoon in the presence of the two Destil men. My stomach roiled into a tight knot. I set aside my fork and swallowed hard, hugging myself. "I-I'm not feeling so well…the eggs…"

Mother's sharp glance made me grimace, and I closed my eyes, swaying a bit in my seat for good measure.

"I f-feel like I'm going to p-puke," I sputtered as though bile already coated my tongue.

"Bathroom!" Her shrill voice made me wince even harder. "Don't you dare vomit in here. The housekeeper will never be able to rid the room of the stench before our luncheon!"

Hand over my mouth, I sprinted from her presence—but I held back a grin rather than spewing my breakfast across the floor. There was no way in hell she would let me out of my bedroom for the rest of the day. The chance I would embarrass her by puking all over her company? Give her a stomach bug?

I'd gained my freedom for the day.

Still smiling, I shut myself in my room and flopped onto my bed.

Yeah, safe…but only for two weeks until the Destil men would return to Anchorage.

4

Gideon

I hadn't been introduced to Ingrid when she'd been down in the lower forty-eight for business, but the second Dad's eyes gleamed while telling me he'd met a rich woman, I knew I would be uprooted.

More like he took a chainsaw to the tree trunk of my life and toppled me into a pile of shit.

We drove up to Alaska to stay just two weeks after having dinner with Ingrid and her daughter. A small moving truck with all our belongings from California packed in tight carried us far from the sunshine and into the frigid cold. Dad had sold off most of the shit that had belonged to his ex-wife three years earlier, but seeing as how he loved to play the stock market—and lose—with whatever he didn't gamble away, he'd become desperate, leaving us with next to nothing.

Not even a goddamn car.

Sure, we had nice threads, name brand shit, but little else.

I wondered if Ingrid knew or if Dad was so good in bed she didn't care he brought nothing to their relationship beyond a grand facade and his dick.

Same as her stuck-up bitch of a mom, Addilyn didn't give me the time of day while I helped the house staff unload the truck. Her best friend, Jenny, however, couldn't keep her eyes off me as I carried box after box up the winding stairs leading to the second floor.

Eventually I sweated enough that I tore off my sweatshirt, and my t-shirt plastered to my upper body, giving the curious girl an eyeful.

I'll admit—her stares stroked my ego. Made something about that first day in our new home not so bad after all.

The bedroom I'd been assigned shared a bathroom with Addilyn. A fucking Jack and Jill bathroom of all things. Talk about a dangerous situation —of the best kind for me. Like a sick fuck, I hoped she didn't understand the need for locks. Maybe I would get lucky and catch her naked and wet from the shower a time or two before she learned to always lock doors against horny bastards who would love to steal the purity Ingrid had bragged about.

At least there was no door direct to the hallway

so Dad couldn't *oops* in on her like he used to do to the last girl. God rest her young soul.

Jenny ended up sleeping over even though it was a school night, and I could hear the girls giggling in the bathroom while getting ready for bed. I'd gotten most of my shit put away and had zero fucking wish to go downstairs and socialize with Dad and Ingrid, so I did what any pervert in my shoes would do.

Ear pressed to the door, I listened in on the younger girls' conversation.

The princess and her friend whispered low enough I only caught my name twice. Hot and gray sweatpants were mentioned, then V-card—that was definitely Jenny's voice—and Addilyn's fake gagging noises immediately after.

Grinning, I carefully tried the door handle—locked, damnit.

The toilet flushed. Water ran.

Seconds later, the lock beneath my hand clicked free.

I waited for the noise of her bedroom door snicking shut before letting myself into the bathroom they'd vacated and filling my lungs with the scent of female and toothpaste. Unlike my sis, I left the door unlocked.

Let her walk in while I showered and jerked off. Maybe she'd get caught like a deer in headlights and watch me blow my load while I groaned out her name.

Dick officially hard and dripping for some much-needed action, I climbed into the glass enclosure and used her peach-scented conditioner to lube up my dick. I didn't bother being quiet as my spunk shot out past my fist and disappeared down the drain a few minutes later.

Maybe the little virgins on the other side of the door were sick fucks like me and listened in. Maybe my groans and grunts while coming made both girls' panties wet to the point they'd secretly finger themselves beneath their blankets once the lights went out.

Balls emptied and body beat from the long as fuck day, I crashed onto the queen-sized guest bed I got to call my own. At least until late spring.

Unless Ingrid wised up and got sick of Dad's bullshit before he put that platinum band on her left hand.

Fuck, I hoped so.

A few days after New Year's was the date they'd set to get hitched. Dad claimed a quiet affair at the courthouse would be best. He assured her there wasn't a need for a prenup, and she seemed so damn fucking gone on him that I expected she'd agree. He wanted to marry the love of his life and grow old and gray together, I'd heard him whispering to her over the phone before we'd even visited Alaska that first time.

Lying asshole.

Kept me close to her though. The snobby princess I feigned indifference toward. The too-young thing I shouldn't have fantasized about sticking my dick into while jerking off. The tits I'd imagined while shooting my spunk in the shower. The mouth I saw in my dreams before waking up hard as hell and ready to bust a nut the next morning.

Fucking Addilyn Reed. Only fifteen, not legally fuckable in the state of Alaska, but all woman and quickly becoming a hated obsession.

She put on that goddamn tiny plaid skirt for school. Button-down white shirt minus the red-brown stain. Black knee-high socks and Mary Janes. White-blonde curls swaying down to the middle of her back.

A fucking teenage wet dream in the flesh.

My dick ached before we finished our quiet breakfast while Dad and Ingrid sat close, giving each other the kind of eyes that told me they hadn't gotten much sleep the night before. Thank fuck their bedroom lay at the far end of the hall and solid oak doors cut off sound.

They murmured. Silverware clinked.

Addilyn ignored me.

Jenny kept glancing my way, pink flushing her cheeks. The second time I caught her staring, I winked. Her shudder and quick look away brought back that good feeling, but I lusted for Addilyn's attention. I wanted the princess to look at me like that—silly-faced adoration. Stars in her eyes, wishful thinking on her mind.

I'd gladly take her V-card given the chance—stepsibling-to-be status could suck it.

Dad and Ingrid weren't married yet, so not sick, really.

But I wouldn't make it good for her. I'd hurt her, cause her to cry for being the one responsible for my situation. Maybe a hard, selfish fuck would bring her down a couple of notches to where she belonged with the rest of us.

I adjusted myself beneath the table at the thought of having her under my control and turned my mind onto my first day at the high school. While I wouldn't know a soul beyond the princess and Jenny, I didn't give two fucks.

Not even halfway through my senior year and Dad made me switch schools. I'd do my time and head back to where I belonged the second I could. Not making new friends like the ones I'd left behind for the next couple of months would make that retreat ten times easier.

The two girls bundled up in winter coats, hats, and gloves, and I shrugged into a sweatshirt atop my long-sleeve t-shirt.

First day at school, and both Dad and Ingrid wanted to drop us off together like we were some fucking Norman Rockwell family.

Never in a million fucking years. Not unless his paintings added in a taboo theme including the princess and my dick.

"We're going car shopping," Ingrid told me while waiting in the drop-off line, her gaze on mine in the rearview. "I decided a welcome gift would be appropriate for both of you. Your father suggested a Jeep Cherokee, Gideon, and I'll make sure it has all the bells and whistles so you're comfortable. It'll be a good vehicle for the amount of snow we get up here."

Sugary-sweet, her words took a few seconds to compute in my head.

"You're buying me a car?" I asked, needing the clarification and wondering if I'd read the selfish bitch wrong.

"Yes." She smiled in the rearview. "Now that Addilyn has an older brother who can drive, I won't be bothered with taking her to school every morning."

Has an older brother, my ass. I had close to a month before that shit officially happened. And she couldn't be *bothered* to drive her daughter to school?

Nah, I'd read her right.

"Unbelievable," the princess muttered.

"Addilyn Jane!" her mother admonished, her goddamn voice like nails on a chalkboard.

"Darling..." Father touched her cheek with his

knuckles. "These are trying times for all of us—and I know patience is one of your greatest virtues."

Manipulative prick.

I glanced over to find Addilyn peering out the car's window, her chin lifted and shoulders straight. Jenny, sitting between us, squeezed her hand quickly, but the girls didn't make eye contact.

Addilyn was one lucky girl to have such a friend.

"I appreciate the offer," I told Ingrid, turning my focus back on the rearview and offering her the smile Dad would encourage. I'd much rather have given the bitch a piece of my mind over the emotional damage her words caused her daughter.

Forget bitch. Ingrid was one selfish, fucking cunt of a woman—even if she shared her money in a way that benefited me.

Having Addilyn in my vehicle every morning, alone with me where I could annoy the shit out of her…

That, I could fucking handle.

Hunched inside my sweatshirt and cursing myself for not thinking to buy a heavy coat, I followed along after Jenny and Addilyn as they hurried toward the school, our exhales escaping our lips like San Francisco's fog.

Alaska's cold weather sucked ass, and not in the good way with a little tongue action.

A few kids lingered along the wide stairs leading

into the main entrance, one blond guy leaving his group of friends to open the door for Addilyn.

"Hey, Addy," he said, giving me a quick glance. "This your new brother?"

So, she'd been talking about me.

I smirked at the back of her head, hands shoved into my jeans' pockets.

"Yes," she answered while stepping past him into the school's foyer. The open door let out a blast of warm air. "Devon, Gideon. Gideon, Devon," she said over her shoulder.

We both nodded, a quick sizing up of each other taking place like all guys our age did.

Preppy. Not loaded though. Decent enough looking kid, one who probably had his sights set on the princess if he was opening goddamn doors for her royal ass.

Dream on, motherfucker.

I couldn't have her—but no one else could either, as far as I was concerned. At least, not until I jetted back to the sunshine where I could *live* and tap whatever ass I wanted. Then, I wouldn't give two shits what happened to the snobby bitch and her cunt of a mother.

Jenny followed after Addilyn, and I paused, grabbing hold of the door above Devon's shoulder. I had an easy four inches on him, but glancing around, I realized my six-two appeared out of the norm.

Fine by me.

"After you," I told him, motioning him in behind the girls with my chin, needing to see how he behaved around my sis before making a final decision on his character.

"Thanks, Gid." He grinned, fucking punched my arm, and loped after the girls.

A muscle ticked in my jaw.

Gid? The fuck?

He sidled up to Addilyn as if he belonged there, shoulder bumping hers like they were some chummy pals or shit. Whatever he said got lost in the sea of high schoolers and raised voices, but she smiled up at him with a look I hadn't yet seen on her face.

Sweet.

Fucking interested.

Like a wet mouth sucked on my dick, I thickened over the sight even as my hands fisted to pop Devon in the face.

Fucking hell.

"Office is down there," Jenny said, tugging on my sleeve and pulling my focus off the pair walking too damn close for my liking. If only Jenny's smile had the same effect on my libido as Addilyn's.

"Thanks, kiddo." I winked, flashed my dimples, and turned toward my first stop of the day. That didn't keep me from watching Addilyn and her little friend disappear down the hallway. If I found out that Devon shit put his hands or mouth anywhere near her body, I'd take him apart piece by fucking piece.

The fuck is wrong with me?

Scowling, I pushed into the office, reminding myself I hated her and that my lust for my soon-to-be-sis was unhealthy as fuck. My messed-up libido came from going without pussy since the night before we left California. Couldn't remember the blonde girl's name, but her heart-shaped face reminded me of Addilyn's.

My brain went with my dick and didn't get the memo over my growing forbidden obsession.

I stalked after Addilyn's ass all damn day. Couldn't fucking help myself.

Stared like a damn creeper every time I caught sight of her in the hallway. With no Dad around, I didn't bother hiding the want from my eyes because it turned her cheeks a shade of pink that made my dick hard.

While sitting down across from her to eat lunch in the cafeteria, my unwavering attention caused the pulse in her neck to thrum. I wanted to feel it beneath my hands. Her nipples beaded into hard buds beneath her thin bra and button-down, and I wanted to close my teeth over them and pull tight until she slapped at my head and shrieked.

Fucking wanted her to the point I didn't bother talking to any of her girlfriends at the table. Not even Jenny who shuddered whenever I brushed my knee against hers. An easy lay if I got too desperate. Hell, taking Addilyn's best friend's V-card would probably piss her the hell off.

I didn't speak a word to Jenny, but I gave her a long, second look, deciding her apple-sized tits and thick lips would do. My stare caused her face to flush.

And brought a scowl to Addilyn's lips.

I smirked in reply to which she flounced her hair and huffed.

Devon Bradshaw didn't share our lunch period, but he handed her a note in the hallway afterward. My hands fisted at my sides. That earned him another one of her smiles that lit up her face and bathed him with the golden rays of sunshine I lusted after.

Other girls offered themselves to me throughout the day, their eyes promising whatever the hell I wanted to give—or take. The chick sitting beside me in physics class slid me a note that outright stated she'd suck my cock.

Didn't even get a twitch out of said cock.

A severe scowl I'd learned to emulate from Dad shut her down.

My dick only got hard for Addilyn, the young girl who pretended to hate me, the princess who thought I was beneath her.

Fuck, what I wouldn't do to *be* beneath her.

And I wasn't the only one to think that. She had a

couple guys sniffing after her like bloodhounds, hot on the trail of young, virginal pussy.

But Devon was the worst of the lot. Fucking fluttering his fingers at her as we headed out to Dad waiting by a shiny new Cherokee just like Ingrid had promised.

"Nice wheels," I told him, catching the keys he tossed me as we drew near.

"Be sure to thank Ingrid when we get home," he said with a wink. Gambling asshole, but he always figured out a way to keep us comfortable. That fact still didn't make me feel any warm fuzzies for the bastard.

"Will do." And I would. Couldn't be a completely ungrateful prick toward her even though I wanted to.

"So, who's Devon and what's he to you?" I asked Addilyn while sliding behind the wheel and fixing my rearview mirror onto her face in the back.

Dad glanced at me from the passenger, but I didn't look his way as he shut his door.

Pink stained Addilyn's cheeks. "He's just a friend," she muttered, turning away from me and clicking her seatbelt into place.

I brought the engine to life, but the topic kept me from grinning at my new wheels. "Seems like he wants to be a hell of a lot more than that."

"Does your mother know about this young man?" Dad asked with a tone that suggested he thought he was some sort of authority figure in her life, but I knew where his disapproval stemmed from. Jealousy —same shit that had my hands itching to form fists.

"Yes, Mother is well aware of Devon," Addilyn snipped. "And she approves of him too. He's Sheriff Bradshaw's son."

A preppy, popular sheriff's son who smiled so damn much he made my own face hurt. Definitely good enough for my princess, her voice and tilted chin claimed.

Motherfucker.

Scowling, I pulled out of the school parking lot and reversed the directions I'd kept track of that morning while Ingrid had driven us to school. Dad asked about school, his voice kind as he angled in his seat to better see Addilyn.

I answered with one-worded grunts, and the princess didn't do much more either, huddling against the door, arms wrapped around herself.

Smart girl.

Dad eventually gave up trying to converse with two moody teenagers who obviously had jack shit to say about their day.

Ingrid met us in the foyer, her smile annoying the hell out of me. "Sweetheart, I missed you!" She kissed Dad, snuggling against him like he'd been gone a week instead of the short time it took to drive all of five miles to the high school.

While I'd have loved to leave them to it, I paused

long enough to thank her for the car she'd bought for me.

"My pleasure," she purred—but kept her focus on Dad instead of me.

What the fuck ever.

Addilyn escaped up the stairs, and I followed on her heels, loving the extra inch of skin I got to see from being lower than her.

I wondered if Dad watched her too, the sick fuck.

5

Addilyn

Having to share a bathroom, having Gideon's body wash bottle sitting in my shower, *and* having his damn clothes falling short of the dirty laundry basket pissed me off.

But, oh the scent of that body wash…grass or something woodsy with a hint of sweetness that reminded me of my favorite candy, Swedish Fish. I sniffed it the next morning, filling my lungs—and frowning over the tingles between my thighs. He'd been nothing but a pain in my ass at school the day before, his scowls scaring off people who would have befriended and welcomed him to Anchorage.

If nothing else, he seemed hell-bent on keeping everyone except me at arm's length.

He even sneered and showed his teeth each time Devon caught up to me in the hallways. While he obviously felt the need to protect me, I needed protection from *him*. He stood close enough to brush against me every chance he got. He stalked after me through the halls. He stared at me in ways that brought on the goosebumps—even when I couldn't even see him, I could feel him.

Watching.

Waiting for a guy to touch me so he could finally hit someone with those fists constantly hanging at the ready by his sides.

Day one alone in his new, shiny Cherokee, and we drove to school in silence for all of thirty seconds before he started in on me.

"Nice car your mom bought me."

"Yeah," I forced a reply, hurt all over again by the fact Mother would spend that kind of money on a boy she hardly knew—all so she wouldn't have to be *bothered* by taking me to school anymore. Mom hadn't ever loved me that I could tell, but since Mr. Destil had made an appearance in her life, that fact had only become more evident. More hurtful.

"I think she might like me or something," Gideon went on to goad me.

That remark didn't require a response.

"Must be the dimples," he continued, and I rolled my eyes. "They always get me what I want."

He wouldn't get anything from me, pretty face with dimples or not.

"Then flash them while begging my mother to

break things off with your father so we can go back to the way they were before you two showed up."

His chuckle caused my eyebrows to furrow.

"I don't think so, princess. While the weather up here sucks, the new bedroom, shared bathroom, new car—kinda cool, really. I'm feeling like a spoiled rich boy."

And two weeks earlier, he hadn't been pleased about moving north.

Whatever.

Hands folded on my lap, I stared straight ahead, deciding to ignore him for the remainder of the ride.

"Hey, princess." His voice didn't hold a trace of teasing or sarcasm, but I refused to acknowledge him. "A word of advice?" he continued anyway. "My dad is full of shit. Don't be drawn in by his lies. He doesn't care about anyone but himself."

I huffed a snort. That sounded like my mother— except for the nice wheels she'd bought for him. But I kept my lips clamped shut about her gift giving too. We didn't need to go all bonding and shit over our selfish parents and what we really thought about them.

A few minutes later, Gideon mentioned Jenny making eyes at him at lunch the day before.

I didn't respond, even though something ugly had twisted in my stomach when he'd checked her out. Even worse, she ignored how I'd told her he was a jackass and melted beneath his stare.

He bragged about a girl in his class asking if she could suck his cock.

That bit of news twitched my lips downward, but I didn't reply. Rumor had it, the young Spanish teacher got caught staring at his ass. She'd probably suck his cock too, given the chance. Hell, half the school, guys included, would love to get on their knees for my gorgeous, breath-stealing stepbrother.

Jackass.

"I'll bet," he said while pulling into the parking lot, "if you let me slide that stick out of your ass, you wouldn't be such a bitch."

Eyebrow raised, I turned my head, giving him my best bitch face.

"Goddamn, you're hot." He grinned, flashing his dimples, sending a rush of heat to my cheeks. "All sweet pussy cat around your mom, but spitfire for me." Shaking his head, he parked and adjusted his groin with a groan. "Makes my dick hard."

Holy shit did he unsettle me in the worst way possible.

"Stay away from me today," I snipped, my insides fluttering while I yanked open the passenger door.

"Not a chance in hell, princess."

Jenny waited at the top of the stairs with Devon, her glance wandering over my shoulder to the jackass my mother had basically leashed me to. I could *feel* his damn stare on my backside.

"Hey, Addy," she said at the same time Devon did.

Like always, he pulled open the door with a love-struck smile. I flashed him a forced one along with a thank you before walking into the crowded foyer.

"See you after second period," I told him and started off toward Jenny's and my homeroom.

Jenny's stare lingered on my face as she scrambled to move in beside me as though her feet had gotten snagged while checking out Gideon and his artfully mussed hair.

"What?" I snapped.

"You didn't give it to him your first night beneath the same roof, did you?"

"Gross." I went with my auto-reply for whenever she talked about Gideon and how much she wanted to climb his naked body like a tree.

"Both parents tucked in their bedroom, completely immersed in one another, Gideon a mere bathroom away, and you didn't let him have his way with you?" She laughed, elbowing me hard enough I sidestepped to keep from stumbling.

"The hell, Jenny?"

"Stepbrother or no, I'd hand over my V-card to him without hesitation if he looked at me the way he stares at you." Jenny snapped her gum, and I didn't bother responding. She'd said those words quite a few times since meeting him.

Kids our age didn't have much to do over the long winter evenings, and I'll admit Gideon was hot enough to make me fantasize about that very thing the night before while lying in bed—even if it was disgusting and I planned on someone ten times more appropriate for all my firsts.

A lush shiver licked down my spine, and I didn't need to turn to know he watched me. He hadn't been kidding about being protective, and while I hated to admit it, his actions almost…endeared him to me a bit regardless of the crap he'd given me on the way to school. But like Jenny had said about the way he looked at me…

"He's a fucking creep," I muttered, remembering his heated stares over dinner while our parents ignored us and I attempted to ignore him.

"Still. I'd give it up to him without hesitation."

I snorted a laugh. "Horny bitch."

"You know it." Jenny linked her arm through mine. "Have you stolen a t-shirt from his dirty hamper yet?"

"Gross."

She laughed, and my lips quirked up for real for the first time in almost twenty-four hours.

By Friday, Gideon finally had enough with guys getting all up in my space.

Devon sauntered my way at the end of the day with a little shoulder bump, sticking closer than usual. The second I felt the energy licking over my skin that announced Gideon's arrival, a different sort of goosebumps broke out over my arms.

I turned in time to see Gideon step in, chest to chest with Devon, hard enough the locker door beside mine clanged from the contact with his backside.

"You need to back the fuck off, let the princess breathe air that isn't tainted by your stench," Gideon growled, hands hanging like clubs at his sides, ready to whack-a-mole my friend down.

"Who the fuck do you think you are?" Devon shot back, shoving at Gideon—and not moving him an inch. "My father's sheriff in this town, and all it'll take is one word from me to land you in trouble."

"I don't give a shit who your dad is." Gideon towered over him, his shoulders hunched and his entire body vibrating. "Leave my sister alone."

"She isn't your sister yet, dickhead." Devon didn't cower physically, but his voice gave away his fear of the big bad wolf.

Gideon eased up a bit and glanced over at me, his attention roaming from my narrowed eyes, down to my toes, and back up, lingering on my traitorous beaded nipples. "Got that right."

All sorts of suggestive inflections filled those last three words, and I wrapped my arms around my books in front of me to hide what he and his hooded gaze caused. "Back off, Gideon. You can't just go threatening my friends for no damn reason—especially the sheriff's son," I said, my tone firm.

Surprisingly, he did as told—and Devon ambled away, muttering a few curses.

"You should keep guys like that at arm's length, princess," Gideon said, his voice low and rumbling straight to my core even though his words sent heat flaring through my belly. "You can't let them step all up in your face like that. They need to show you respect."

"Like you show me respect?" I damn near spit at him. "I ought to kick *you* in the balls."

Gideon leaned down, stealing my breath. His blue eyes glinted as he angled toward my ear. "I'd rather you sucked them," he whispered, his hot exhale shivering across my skin.

"Jackass," I whispered fiercely, disgusted over how my pulse throbbed between my thighs.

"*Princess.*" He ambled off like he hadn't a care in the world, and since I had zero wish to walk home in the flying snow, I followed after him, the heat rushing through me in a terrifying mixture of anger and arousal I didn't know how to handle.

6

Gideon

The weeks passed cold as fuck, the sky dark as fuck, and my frown permanently in fucking place.

Alaska sucked, and Ingrid seemed more in love with Dad with every passing day. Ruined my goddamn breakfast more than one morning, having them acting like their worlds revolved around one another.

I saw Dad's straying gaze even if Ingrid didn't.

He might be caught up in his love affair and the plans to weasel his way legally into her life, but he'd stray eventually. The idea of Addilyn was too damn addictive for him not to.

Christmas morning, Ingrid spoiled the hell out of us—daughter included. New iPhones, new threads, a flatscreen TV for my room...fuck yeah, I thanked her for that shit even though her money made me jealous as hell—and rekindled resentment inside me toward Dad.

He hadn't ever been one for giving a single gift or two, and once he gambled all our money away, I never got jack shit.

The following days of Christmas break?

Fucking torture.

Addilyn and me beneath the same roof every goddamn day. Dad and Ingrid in and out of the house, both heading to her offices downtown. She'd taken him into her Reed Enterprises, giving him a seat on the board, a title, and all that shit.

She also agreed to the no prenup idea. Stupid bitch, but whatever. It'd be her funeral someday— not mine—that lined Dad's pockets. I wondered if he'd give me a cut or leave me high and dry. Knowing him, it'd be the latter, but I told myself I might get lucky for a change.

A few nights before New Year's, the two of them went out to eat, their last official date before saying "I do."

That left me alone with the princess who locked herself up in her room.

I kept my bathroom door open—just in case she wanted a peek of me sprawled on my bed that sat right in line with the damn thing. Direct view. I watched the clock while flicking through channels on my new flatscreen, one arm propped behind my head.

At nine-twenty, I flicked off the TV, dimmed my overhead lights, and stripped down, keeping my sheet mid-thigh. I pulled the silk panties I'd stolen from the hamper earlier in the day from beneath my pillow. Hard dick in hand, I settled in, hoping she wouldn't derail from her usual nine-thirty nightly routine of readying for bed.

A few sniffs of her dirty panties, a couple of leisurely strokes along my dick, and thoughts of her mouth wrapped around my dick caused pre-cum to ooze from the slit. I twirled that shit around the throbbing head, smearing it down over my length, my hips rising to meet my fist.

Fuck, jerking off to thoughts of Addilyn, to her musky scent made me want to blow faster than usual.

I squeezed my balls to keep from shooting early, my dick pulsing in my hand.

"Come on, princess," I hissed through clenched teeth, focusing on her door on the other side of the bathroom while wrapping her dirty panties around my dick to lessen the skin-on-skin friction.

Two more strokes of silk along my length pulled a groan from my chest, and thank fuck, her door handle turned.

Head down, she walked into the bathroom, firmly tying a flannel robe around her waist.

I hooded my eyes and groaned louder, sucking my lower lip between my teeth.

She stumbled to a stop, her head whipped up—and she fucking froze like a goddamn deer.

Jesus, fuck.

I squeezed my base, holding my length straight up in the air to let her see the precum ooze from my slit. "You look like you want this," I rasped out. "Come on over and ride my dick, princess."

Pink flushed her high cheek bones, and another groan rumbled through my chest.

"I'm only fifteen," she whispered, attempting for sass and falling so damn short I wanted to laugh at her attempt.

"Soon to be sixteen," I reminded her, moving my dick back and forth with my hand, even though I knew there was no way in hell I'd tempt her into climbing aboard.

"Are those...my panties?" Her voice rose at the end, clearly headed toward hysterics.

I grinned. "Pulled them out of the hamper this morning. Still warm. Still damp from your pussy. Got a fresh whiff of your musk. Been thinking about it all goddamn day."

"You're sick," she spat out with a little more heat —but stared at my hand as I slid it up and over my tip again. The schlicking noise of more pre-cum coating my fingertips tingled my balls.

"And I'll bet your wet," I grunted the words with assurance, lifting my hips to fuck my fist through her panties.

Mute, lips parted, and chest heaving, she met my gaze.

Blue eyes hazed with innocent lust—fuck how I wanted to ruin her mascara, streak her cheeks with blackened tears.

"If I slid my fingers between your thighs, what would I find, Addilyn?" I fucked through my grasp again, imagining shoving my dick into her throat, ready to blow my spunk all over my chest while she watched. "Hmm? *Are* you wet for my dick, princess?"

"Y-you're sick." Face full-on red, she rushed across the bathroom—and slammed my goddamn door shut.

My balls exploded, and I grunted with every ribbon of sticky white spurting over my chest and abs.

"Fucking hell…" I gritted my teeth as the last two dribbles leaked from my slit. "Jesus."

I sank back, chuckling at the ceiling, knowing Addilyn would never again open her bathroom door without peeking first.

Uptight little princess definitely needed that stick removed from her ass—if only she'd let me slide it out and replace the length with my dick.

I ended up stroking myself to climax minutes

later to thoughts of her tight rosebud stretching around my girth, her tears soaking her pillow—because no fucking way would I take her in my bed. It'd be on her sheets, her virginal mattress, where I would fuck the attitude right out of her and show her she was just as depraved as me.

7

Addilyn

I knew what Gideon did the second I caught sight of him lying back on his bed, and I stared a few seconds too long at his hand, slick and glistening in the lowered lights. He took advantage of my pause to tease me. Wrapping my panties around his length and jerking off in them.

Jackass.

My pulse thrumming in my ears, I stared at myself in the bathroom mirror, my hands in a white-knuckle clench on the vanity's edge.

He used my panties—dirty ones from the basket behind me.

Totally gross, and yet my core pulsed at the thought.

I'd never seen a guy masturbate before. Never saw a guy's penis outside of drawings in my health class and a few pictures I'd peeked at on my new cell when Jenny had slept over the night after Christmas.

Red fused my cheeks, and I cupped them in my hands, quietly cursing myself, cursing Gideon.

I hated that he made my insides ache with longing Mother said only older women ought to feel.

I hated how the way he bit his lower lip churned up my mind over breaking my determination to wait for my sweet sixteen kiss too.

I hated that Mother showed him as much attention as she did me and thought she could earn his appreciation and respect with gifts.

Lips tight, I yanked open the top vanity drawer and grabbed my brush. A few harsh strokes straightened a bit of the natural curl to my hair, and I once again cursed—but this time at Mother for not allowing me to cut my hair into a short bob like I'd always wanted.

Long hair was beautiful, she claimed. Feminine and graceful when pinned up for special events. Classy rather than whorish.

Chit'n Chat never said anything like that about hair styles, and her words made me wonder what Mother had been taught as a kid—not enough to ask though. The last thing I needed was more "woe is me" bullshit from the woman who was supposed to love me unconditionally.

All but growling, my eyes stinging over the relentless knots, I tossed the brush away and finished with my nightly routine. The temptation to keep Gideon locked out of the bathroom had me nibbling my lower lip while studying his door, but in the end, I relented and unlocked his before scampering back to my bedroom—and locking mine from the outside.

Heart once more pounding, I stared at my door and waited, knowing he would want to wash up the mess he'd made.

I remembered hearing his moans the first night he'd moved in. Jenny and I had been wide-eyed and staring at one another as he'd taken care of himself in the shower. We had giggled afterward, but I'd never been able to rid my mind of the image I'd conjured. Every time my ears caught the hint of him doing it again, that night came to mind.

And now I have the real thing to imagine.

Blowing out a heavy exhale, I turned down my lights, shook off my robe to leave at the foot of my bed, and crawled beneath my covers. I lay on my back, staring at the ceiling, knowing I wouldn't ever be able to sleep.

Jenny was a night owl, so I grabbed my cell off my bedstand.

Me: **Awake still?**

She called rather than texting a reply. "Did you give it to him?"

I rolled my eyes. "Never, but I caught him jerking off," I whispered, biting back a giddy smile.

"No. Way."

"Seriously. With the panties I wore yesterday."

"What?"

"He must have gotten them out of the dirty laundry."

"Oh my God," she moaned, and I could see her flopping back onto her bed as an oomph noise filled my ear. "Tell me. Vivid details, please. How thick, how long. Veins and all."

I tried to fulfill my best friend's fantasy but couldn't find the right words to adequately describe the vision of his hips lifting, abs flexing, the small noises rumbling in his chest as his hand made a wet sound while sliding up and down his length.

My core pulsed, and I closed my eyes, silently reminding myself that I hated Gideon Destil, that the desire I felt for him was shameful.

"I'm so jealous," Jenny whined. "Can I sleep at your place tomorrow night? We can leave his door open earlier in the day on purpose and maybe we'll both get lucky later."

"No!" I barked out with a laugh, my insides still jittery enough that my voice shook.

"Come on, Addy! I'll leave my panties on the vanity for him if you don't want him using yours again."

That ugly feeling in my stomach roused to life, and my laughter cut off. "No."

"Well at least let me come over. We can snuggle, get sick off Swedish Fish, and watch Stolen. It released on Blue-Ray yesterday."

The stalker movie we'd seen over the summer where the anti-hero kidnapped the woman he'd obsessed over had been all we'd talked about for months on end.

"That was so hot," I said, remembering how much the movie had heated me up. I'd felt strange, weird over being turned on by thoughts of being kidnapped and tied up for some asshole's pleasure, but after Jenny admitted to it first, I admitted I did too.

We'd had good laughs and a long discussion over Stockholm syndrome. Not that we actually wanted it to happen for real.

"Could you imagine being taken like that?" I murmured anyway, wanting to reminisce to rid my mind of my stepbrother and all the talk of panties and what he did with them. "Tied up to some guy's bed, being held against your will?" I liked the shiver licking over my skin a little too much.

"We're sick," Jenny said with a quiet laugh.

"It's not sick—it does happen," I stated. "Guy kidnaps girl, girl falls for guy, and they end up having sex in every position there is."

"Every position." Jenny snorted.

"I'm serious!"

"Name a few."

"Missionary. Doggy style."

"Yeah? And?" she prompted when I hesitated, wracking my brain.

I frowned. "Okay, so I don't have much knowledge, but I've got a good imagination."

"Same, girl."

"And every fantasy showcases my stepbrother, am I right?" I asked, rolling my eyes and hating the return of that weird twist in my stomach.

"Damn right."

"You're sick."

"You're an idiot for not…what'd he say? Climbing up on his dick and going for a ride?"

I imagined straddling his trim waist, his rippling abs with the dark line of hair beneath my fingertips. The hairs on my neck stood on end as though he'd walked in my room, but a quick glance around showed it empty of anyone but me. "Maybe you better sleep over tomorrow night," I whispered while lying back and closing my eyes, "and we can use Google to teach us a few things."

"I might have done some searching on my phone already."

My eyelids popped open. "You dirty sneak!"

"Well…"

I could imagine her shrug, the embarrassment turning her face red. I also felt cheated a bit. Jenny and I did everything together, always had since we met in kindergarten. "I'm going to hang up now and browse to my heart's content."

"Don't you dare without me!"

"You did it to me!" I shot back, grinning and burrowing under my blankets.

"Fine," Jenny said with a sigh. "Look up some stuff and bookmark the good links to show me tomorrow. I'll see what I can find too."

Grinning, I agreed, and a few seconds later, I pulled my covers over my head, opened an incognito tab, and went bug-eyed at what I brought up on my screen with a few taps of my fingertips. Mostly drawings of sexual positions but some images of real people as well. Videos.

Lower lip between my teeth, I clicked on an image that took me to a pornography site and promptly fell down a rabbit hole of arousal and fantasy. Thick dicks, wet and gaping holes. Ropes and swats that left handprints on ass cheeks and made my own backside tingle with curiosity. Dirty words and cries when gushing around fingers and stabbing lengths.

Mother would be horrified by what I stared at, what she'd always warned me away from in order to remain pure—but I couldn't keep from clicking. Watching. Gulping and gasping.

When I finally cleared my history, shut off my cell, and set it aside, an hour had passed.

Wetness smeared inside my panties, and shame heated my cheeks. But I needed something...release, no matter how wrong Mother claimed it was.

I burrowed beneath my blankets again and slid my fingertips under the band. Slick and hot to the touch, my core ached for more than the finger I pushed inside me.

I wanted something thicker, a real-life penis like the one Gideon had held in hand. Imagining him shoving deep into my body, my hands held in his tight fists overhead, his muscles flexing with every thrust like I'd seen on various videos...

Panting, I rode the wave of my fantasy, bringing myself to climax. Not nearly as good as I expected the real thing would be, but I had no wish to fulfill my fantasy.

My body might lust for my stepbrother, but he would be the last jackass on the face of the earth I would ever admit to wanting.

8

Gideon

The little princess had a kidnapping fantasy. She'd locked me out—yeah, I tried her door after busting my nut the second time and leaving her cum-soaked panties on the vanity—so I listened in on her conversation with Jenny. The idea of stealing Addilyn away and giving her that fantasy hit me like a punch to the gut and a shot of adrenaline to the balls.

I jerked off for a third time that night, wishing I could fulfill that one for her, going deeper into darkness with each thought.

She would be bound for my pleasure because it sure as fuck wouldn't be for hers.

Bending her over while standing, wrists tied to her ankles so I could take her ass without a struggle. She'd end up so damn wrecked I'd have to hold her upright until I finished using her body to finally find release in her tight hole.

Begging for me to stop because I hurt her. Her lips trembling, mascara-stained tears, eyes red from crying...lipstick smeared from gagging around my dick...fuck yeah.

Only a dribble oozed from my chafed length over those final thoughts, and my balls ached from draining them dry. Since I'd left her panties in the bathroom beside her toothbrush for her to find come morning, I grabbed a tissue off my bedstand to wipe up.

I passed the fuck out minutes later and dreamed about kidnapping the little princess, keeping her secluded, without social media, her friends, all her money, and making her my sex slave.

My body rejuvenated overnight, and I woke up with a raging hard-on.

"What the absolute fuck!" Addilyn's curses rang through the bathroom door, reminding me of what I'd done the night before. "Disgusting...foul... damnit, Gideon! You are so...so *gross!*"

A fist banged on my bathroom door, and smirking, I rolled off the bed and sauntered over, naked, ready to face down the spitting mad woman I wanted kneeling at my feet.

I wrenched the door open. "Morning," I muttered, flashing my dimples, my dick at attention after catching sight of her sleep shorts and camisole that revealed tight buds poking and ready for my teeth.

She glanced down at my bobbing length and quickly turned her head to the side, eyes closed. "You are a disgusting *pig*!" With a flick of her hand, dried, cum-crunchy panties landed against my chest. They fell to the floor, and I bent to pick them up.

"Couldn't help myself," I said, unable to keep from grinning while sniffing the silk to see if any of her musky scent lingered beneath my dried spunk.

"I've moved my hamper into my bedroom," she stated firmly, turning to walk toward her bathroom door without giving me a single glance.

Christ, that ass... She sauntered away, tempting me like no girl ever had.

"So, what am I supposed to jerk off to?" I asked, lazing my palm over the head of my dick. Damp...I smeared that shit down over my length and moaned a bit.

She shivered at the sound, and my grin widened.

"Your own damn underwear!"

"I don't wear any."

Addilyn stumbled and grabbed her doorjamb but still wouldn't face me. "Disgusting."

"It isn't disgusting for the woman wanting easy access to my dick."

"Well that woman isn't me!"

I squeezed my balls with her ruined panties,

tugging them down a bit. "I won't ever turn you away if you change your mind, princess."

"Sick," she spat as though she was so much better than me.

Her hand grabbed hold of the door to slam it shut.

"Did you touch yourself last night?" I shot out, loving when she paused. "Get off to thoughts of your dirty panties wrapped around my dick?"

The rapid rise and fall of her chest said it all.

"Yeah, you did. Damn." I squeezed my balls again as a bead of pre-cum welled at my slit. "Think I'll jerk off to that image in my head."

She escaped—but not without a quick glance at my groin—slamming the door behind her. The click let me know she had zero wish to continue our conversation, even if her eyes had suggested otherwise.

I climbed into the shower and rubbed one out while imagining her slender fingers shoving into her tight hole the night before all because she'd gotten an eyeful of my dick. I groaned a little louder than necessary when shooting my spunk up over my abs, wondering how wet I made the panties she had on beneath her sleep shorts.

Too fucking bad I wouldn't be able to sneak them from the hamper anymore for a deep lungful of her musk before hitting the shower every morning.

9

Addilyn

Not fifteen minutes into our girls' night watching Stolen and Gideon sauntered into our mini movie theatre, the usual energy of him in close proximity raising the hairs on my arms.

"Get out!" I snapped and shoved popcorn into my mouth, pulling my attention off him crossing the threshold back toward the massive flatscreen.

"He's fine, Addy," Jenny said. She patted her side of the sectional. "Come on over here, handsome."

Growling beneath my breath, I scowled at my friend in the dim lighting—the mood we'd set with the overheads.

"Handsome, huh?" He flashed his damn dimples at my friend.

Smirking, she shrugged.

Enter that weird twisting again. Was it…jealousy?

Nope. No way.

Gideon plopped his gray sweats-covered ass down beside her, lounging back and showcasing the bulge he didn't contain with underwear.

My core pulsed at the thought of easy access, and if Jenny's side-eye glances were any indication, she thought of the exact same thing I did.

The feeling in my stomach grew.

Okay, so definitely jealousy. I didn't like how he sat close to her, his thigh a breath away from hers. I also didn't like how she shifted as though getting comfortable—brushing her leg against his and leaving it there.

His T-shirt went tight over his chest and shoulders as he stretched an arm across the back of the couch. Around her damn shoulders, even if he didn't rest on them.

I imagined Jenny swooned, but I turned back to the screen, fighting off the ridiculous green-eyed monster and the images of what his body looked like beneath his sweats and shirt. How his muscles strained with every upward thrust of his hips, sliding his length through his fist. My panties.

"Stolen?" Gideon asked, bringing my wayward mind back to the theatre.

"Yep," Jenny answered while I shifted to relieve the damp discomfort between my thighs.

"Isn't this that movie about a kidnapping and the captor falling for the guy who stole her out of her damn bed?"

"Yep." Jenny again.

Gideon chuckled, and I could feel his stare even though I refused to give him the time of day.

I shoved more popcorn into my mouth, staring hard at the images flashing over the screen.

"You two are seriously getting off on this shit, aren't you?" he asked.

"Shut up!" I yelped around my mouthful of food, a few pieces spewing from my lips.

"It *is* hot," Jenny admitted quietly.

"Pervs." Gideon laughed. "I'll bet you've been Googling the shit out of the stuff your mommies have been keeping you away from all these years on Addilyn's new cell."

Neither of us said a word, and heat flooded my face.

"Yeah, that's what I thought." His tone suggested arrogance. "So do you finger each other once you're all hot and bothered or take care of yourselves?"

"Sick bastard," I muttered, wishing Mother had heard him say such a thing. But yeah, he got it right on the last part, and the realization he wondered over me touching myself made my core pulse.

"I like guys, thank you very much." Jenny backhanded him in the arm.

"Ouch!" He rubbed at his arm as though she'd

actually hurt him. "Just looking for some dick spanking material. Two young things like you getting all wet over losing your virginal purity… good shit right there."

"Would you please leave," I stated through gritted teeth, finally casting him a glare I wished would burn him to cinders on the spot.

Gideon held my stare with a knowing look, all hooded—hot and full of lust. He blatantly adjusted his groin, squeezing a little more than necessary while moving against Jenny's leg enough that she blatantly stared at his hand wrapped around his balls.

His gaze narrowed at me even further, and I realized I scowled at the two of them. Touching.

I turned away with a huff, feigning indifference I certainly didn't feel.

"Imagine that." He chuckled, and I cursed myself, knowing he noticed my…jealousy. "This kidnapping shit and the scent of turned on pussy filling this room…yeah." Gideon stood, still holding his dick, the jackass. "I think I'll go rub one out now." He sauntered off with a quiet, intentional groan, and Jenny's wide-eyed stare lingered on his ass until the door shut.

Cheeks pink, she finally glanced at me. "What?"

"You still want to climb his body like a tree?" I snapped.

"Oh hell yes," she whispered and clutched a

pillow to her belly, eyes hazed over and clueless to what had gone down between him and I.

My head suddenly ached. "You can have the jackass," I hissed through my clenched teeth, even though the thought of the two of them together made my blood boil. I clicked up the TV volume and grabbed another handful of popcorn, hoping like hell he hadn't really been able to smell the fact the movie, him, and his words about fingering had turned me on.

***

Getting ready at home for the wedding day from hell —and Mother had chosen the most butt-ugly dress in the most hideous color for my skin tone.

Yellow.

A puke yellow, which made no sense, considering how much vomit grossed her out. It wasn't even bright or sunshiny like her usual yellows. More mustard than golden.

I looked like death.

But I still held my chin high and shoulders back while stepping lightly down the stairs toward the foyer below.

Both Gideon and his father waited at the foot, dressed in suits like the first day I'd met them. Mother's soon-to-be husband had stood the test of time in my opinion, even though I still held onto the hope he'd get sick of her—even if his presence made her less of a bitch than normal. A small yellow rose bud was pinned to the lapel of his black suit coat, and he either chose or Mother insisted on the golden tie around his neck.

If only my dress had been closer in color to his tie…

Gideon wore black on black. Fitting for his soul, and damn, did he look mighty fine. Hair artfully mussed. Freshly shaven…and crinkling his nose.

"What the hell color is that dress?" he asked as I neared the foyer's floor.

Heat flooded my face, and I watched my step the rest of the way down. "I hate yellow—it looks hideous on me," I muttered, trusting his dad not to tell my mother what I thought of the dress she'd chosen for me.

"Damn right, it does," Gideon agreed, making me feel ten times worse.

"Thanks for that," I sassed with a sarcastic smile. "As if I don't feel shitty enough already."

"Gideon, go get in the limo while we wait for Ingrid," Lloyd said, his tone not one to be refused.

The jackass hesitated but obeyed his father, and I let out a heavy exhale.

"I hate yellow too," Lloyd stated quietly once the door shut behind Gideon, "but it's your mother's favorite color, and since it's her day…" He shrugged lightly, his coat stretching tight over his shoulders as he smiled down at me with a look in his eyes that suggested a shared secret. "Some things just aren't worth arguing over."

My embarrassment eased a bit.

"If it's any consolation—" he leaned toward me, his voice lowering, eyes not teasing yet full of a sense of lightness I didn't understand "—I think you look absolutely ravishing."

More heat flooded my face, and I found myself smiling for the first time in days. I expected he thought I was like a younger version of the woman he adored, and the idea warmed me. "Thank you."

Lloyd offered a wink and nodded toward the door where one of the house staff held my winter coat. "Go on and bundle up. It's chilly outside."

I shrugged on my coat, ready for the door, and Lloyd's murmured, "Beautiful," turned me back around.

Mother stood at the top of her stairs in her white, silk wedding dress that must've cost a fortune. A beaded bodice hugged her torso, down over the flare of her hips, giving way to sheer material in layers to create a waterfall effect. Bright white as though she was pure like her daughter, but she'd brought enough men into her bed I knew the truth.

I wondered if Lloyd did—then told myself I didn't give a shit.

He'd made his bed in hers and would be stuck with the consequences. I just hoped his kinder character would continue to rub off on Mother enough to make living with her less of a tedious task.

"Darling." Lloyd held her hands and kissed her cheeks. "You look ravishing."

My eyebrows pulling into a frown, I slipped into my coat one of the house staff held for me. Surely I wasn't jealous he used the same compliment on me?

Pushing the strange feelings away by telling myself Lloyd was a fake, I lifted my chin and marched outside, preferring to wait in the cold for Mother and Lloyd rather than climb into the limo with Gideon whose gaze pebbled my skin even though I couldn't see him through the tinted glass.

Jackasses. Both father and son.

$$10$$

Gideon

During the quiet affair at the courthouse, I stared at Addilyn in her hideous dress rather than watch our parents exchange vows and rings. The color didn't do much for the princess, but beyond that? Drop. Dead. Fucking. Gorgeous. White-blonde hair in long ringlets clear to her ass...I wanted to fist those strands while she swallowed my dick. Gagged at my girth, her gloss-slicked lips leaving remnants on my length. She'd glare up at me with all the spitfire I lusted to see in her eyes.

Every adjustment I made to my dick in my dress pants caught her attention, but she didn't give me more than a side eye. Guess I shouldn't have been too quick to spout off my brutally honest thoughts over her bridesmaid dress. But I'd never been one to mince words or lie. She had to know that.

At least I hadn't called her out for the jealousy that had been radiating from her like an August sun off fresh tar when I'd flirted a bit with Jenny. The little princess had clenched her jaw, narrowed her eyes—glared at me with those icy blue orbs I wanted to see lost in need for release.

That, more than anything, was what had me hard as fuck.

And knowing my flirting pissed her off? Easiest and best way to fuel the fire.

Once school started back up, I'd take advantage of that shit. Create a crack between the two girls, the kind that ripped apart with time, the type that would destroy their friendship rather than draw them closer.

Ruin the snob. Bring her down from the holier than thou pedestal she'd put herself on, show her she was flesh and blood like her best friend. Hot for dick—specifically mine, one she saw as below her station.

I gave Addilyn my attention as Dad slid a ring on Ingrid's hand in my periphery.

Pointed chin lifted exposing my official stepsister's neck. Nose aloft, ignoring me…

The pulse thrummed in her carotid. Her nipples hardened beneath that god-awful dress. I wanted to put my hands around her neck and feel the pump of blood beneath my fingertips…

Smirking and chubbing up, I turned back toward the JP as Dad kissed his bride.

Within the hour, we dined in some country club, just the four of us, like a happy little family.

The lovebirds sat beside each other at our table covered with a white linen cloth, real fucking china, and crystal goblets for our water and Ingrid's wine. They discussed their honeymoon down in Cancun they'd leave for in the morning while Addilyn and I ate in mostly silence, her contemplating who the hell knew what—probably still pissy at me for hating her dress and flirting with Jenny—and me thinking about having the house all to myself with the little princess beneath my care for two fucking whole weeks.

Dick swelling at the thought of stalking her ass for a few peeks—fucking perv—I shifted to relieve the ache in my groin. A dip of my hand beneath the linen tablecloth took care of the problem, but I brushed my knee against hers. Intentionally.

Her breath caught in a quiet gasp, and I gave her a side eye of my own, my thoughts going straight to licking her parted lips where traces of peach gloss still clung.

Dad pulled Ingrid close to whisper in her ear, and I took advantage of that shit, running my knuckles along the side of Addilyn's thigh as she reached for her water.

Her hand wrenched to the side to stop me—and

her goblet went flying across the table, most of the ice-cold water splashing over her mom's chest.

Ingrid shrieked, pushing back from the table, her eyes hard as fuck, face red as a cherry. "Addilyn!" She hissed as Dad grabbed a napkin to blot at her cleavage.

"Sorry," Addilyn whispered, shrinking down in her chair as two waiters hurried to our table to help.

"You careless, bumbling…" Ingrid seethed, shoving Dad's hands away to wipe herself up. "How many times have I reiterated proper poise? It's my wedding day, and you've ruined it," she continued, her low, hissing voice so damn degrading even I cringed. "Of all the selfish, petty things to do… Your cell is gone for a month, you jealous little bit—"

"Ingrid, darling," Dad cut her off, closing his hand over hers and offering Addilyn a pitying smile. "I'm sure it was an accident."

I sat in silence, and my gut clenched up tight, Addilyn's trembling beside me hitting like a smack across my face. "It wasn't her fault," I lied, clueless as to why I'd spout off that sort of nonsense.

Dad glared at me as Ingrid whipped her focus my way.

In for a penny… "I bumped her arm as she was reaching for her water."

"Perhaps you should take a bit more care," Dad stated, his voice firm, gaze stern. "Do you see what you've done?"

No, enlighten me, I wanted to tell him with the sneer trying to break free from my lips.

Face still red and splotchy, Ingrid tossed her wet linen napkin onto the table and stood to take stock of her wedding gown. "The silk is ruined." She all but wailed her whisper while peering at Dad.

He shot me another glare. "You've been testy since we moved here, Gideon." He snapped at me, and I knew what was coming even if I didn't deserve it. "If you don't get your act together and accept your fate for the next couple of months, I'll send you home on your eighteenth birthday without a dime to your name."

I wanted to spew that he didn't have a goddamn cent of his own to give me anyway, but I bit my tongue, letting his words help pacify the bitch in white so she'd leave Addilyn alone.

A tear slid down Ingrid's cheek, and Dad turned his attention on her, making shushing noises and promising they would escape soon for two weeks of uninterrupted bliss. Selfish pricks—the both of them. Unfit for parenting.

I glanced over at Addilyn to find her eyes wet with unshed tears. Our gazes collided—and so did something else inside. A connection of recognized shared pain as she peered at me with those big blue eyes.

All animosity blinked out, and I simply stared at a young girl whose heart had without doubt been broken over and over. Same as mine—but I'd become hardened, accepting of the fact I'd never be good enough or live up to my dad's expectations. I was nothing more than a jackass according to her, not letting anyone in, not trusting. Jealousy and anger ruled my mind and actions.

But she…

Addilyn's heart remained soft in areas she kept closed off.

In that moment, I felt she allowed me a glimpse of the real her, allowed me inside because of our shared torment.

Her lips wobbled, but my princess offered me a first real smile with just one corner of her lips quirking upward. She didn't say thank you—not that I'd expected her to. Still, I'd managed to see a piece of her heart.

I nodded in acknowledgement, my chest so damn on fire I couldn't breathe.

11

Addilyn

The second we got home, Mother held up the hem of her skirt and stalked up the stairs. She hadn't spoken to me after returning from the bathroom at the country club, and the rest of the dinner had passed in stifling silence. Even Lloyd's attempts at small talk had fallen short.

I'd ruined Mother's day—or according to Gideon, *he* had.

When our gazes had clashed, something seemed to tie us together in that moment, and I knew why he'd done it. A jackass, sure, but I was starting to think he might actually care for me. He hated how Mother treated me, same as I hated how his father treated him.

I hurried upstairs to get rid of my own dress but

barely kicked my heels off before a soft knock sounded on my door.

Opening it revealed Lloyd. "Can I come in for a quick moment?" he asked quietly.

"Sure." I stepped back, letting him in—but I kept my door swung wide like Mother always insisted upon if someone of the male gender entered my room.

"My apologies, Addilyn" he said, turning to face me, his hands clasped in front of him. His dark eyebrows pulled downward, but no anger rested in his eyes. "Your mother has been so stressed, wanting everything to be perfect for our day."

"It's okay," I whispered, glancing beyond him to the empty hallway and praying Mother didn't see him inside my room.

"Don't worry about the cell phone." Lloyd reached out to squeeze my shoulder. "I promise to calm her tonight and make sure you have your phone in hand before we leave in the morning."

"Thank you." I peered up at him, for the first time thinking that he really wasn't all that bad. He must truly love Mother. I didn't understand how, but I desired that kind of adoration when I got older.

"I hope I find someone who loves me half as much as you do her," I heard myself say.

Lloyd smiled, his eyes full of that same light from earlier. His warm hand fell away from my shoulder. "What about the sheriff's son?"

Devon.

I chewed on the corner of my lip for a second, considering. "Gideon doesn't approve of him hanging around me. He…bullies Devon." My shoulders hitched up in a shrug. "It's not like the poor guy even has a chance to ask me to be his girlfriend—not that Mother would allow such a thing, anyway."

Lloyd studied my face long enough that I shifted on my bare feet, my toes digging into the soft carpet beneath me.

"You need to be careful with my son."

As if I didn't know.

"He beat a kid half to death back in California a few years ago, and he's lucky I had the connections to keep him out of serious trouble."

I stared up at Lloyd. The whole anger management issues I'd heard Mother gossiping about over the phone were a hell of a lot worse than she'd said.

"I promise once he's eighteen and graduated, he'll leave for the south again. Then maybe I can talk your mother into inviting Devon and his family over dinner. His father and I have become close friends in our short time here." Lloyd's face softened with a slow smile. "How would that be?"

My eyes stung. He would never take my real father's place in my life, but maybe he could fill the shoes partway.

"I just want my girls happy," he said.

Happy.

Perhaps I would learn the meaning of that word after all. "I-I'd like that."

Lloyd winked. "Then I'll make it happen."

____

12

Gideon

____

Addilyn avoided me for two full days after our parents left for their honeymoon, so I never got a chance to make sure her mother's outburst over their wedding day dinner hadn't done major emotional damage to my princess.

On day three, she hurried out the front door to hop in my car for her ride to school.

"You okay?" I asked as I pulled out of the driveway, wishing we'd been able to stay shut up the entire two weeks at home.

"Yeah," she replied, breathless from running out the door.

We left it at that for the duration of our ride. We'd had a moment at the bridal dinner that left me floundering a bit. I still hated her attitude toward me, but part of me softened with understanding, knowing she was going through the same shit I was.

Add in our selfish, shared asshole parents, and the instinct to watch over her intensified.

The appearance of Devon at the door, all grinning and eyes only for her after their Christmas break separation, had me clenching my jaw. I wanted to bash his goddamn face in for looking at her like he did. Somehow, I managed to walk away and get through the first two periods without exchanging words with him.

On the way to fourth, I stood down the hall from Addilyn, both of us in our lockers to exchange books.

Some little shit from the football team—captain if I remembered correctly—sidled up to her, leaning in a bit too close.

My gut clenched, and my insides burned in a whole new jealous flare after receiving that smile from her.

I slammed my locker door and strode their way, shoving other little shits out of my path. One kid went tumbling to the floor, but I didn't stop to apologize or help him pick up his scattered papers.

His muttered, 'jerk' would have normally gotten him a bloody nose, but the asshole all up in Addilyn's personal space kept my rage focused.

She saw me first, her eyes widening. Grabbing hold of the asshole's arm, her mouth moved rapidly.

He glanced over his shoulder, took note of my approach, and grinned.

Stupid fuck.

With a wink, he sauntered the other way, escaping before I reached them.

"Would you knock it off with that caveman bullshit?" Addilyn slammed her locker door and glared up at me with sass in her eyes and tone of voice.

My dick twitched, my attention fully taken by her fire. "Goddamn, you make me hard."

She smacked my chest and flounced away, leaving me staring after her and wishing I could grab my dick right there in the hallway.

Letting out a heavy grunted exhale, I turned back around, but the football captain had disappeared into class. I decided to give him a pass for providing me a second of Addilyn's undivided, pissy attention.

After that period, I caught sight of Devon handing a note to my princess when they passed in the hallway. She flashed him that smile I'd only snagged a partial piece of. Liberally. Like she really meant it.

Like he deserved it.

Fucker.

Devon smirked my way. Fucking winked at me, the arrogant little shit.

Same thing happened after sixth period, and I stalked up her ass the second we exited the building out into the cold afternoon.

Wind bit at my face, but I didn't feel it—I was too damn focused on the short skirt the wind blew tight against Addilyn's juicy ass. Couldn't really blame the guys for wanting a taste. With a backside as curvy as that, what hot-blooded male wouldn't?

Fuckers. If anyone so much as touched her…

"Would you just stop," she snapped at me once she slid into my car and slammed the passenger door shut.

"What?" I muttered, glaring while pulling out of my assigned parking spot.

"Being such a jackass!" She snuggled into her heavy coat, knees pressed tight together against the cold.

I eyed thighs that should have been allowed to be covered by pants considering the goddamn frigid as fuck weather. Goosebumps raised areas of her skin, and I gripped the steering wheel tight to keep from reaching over and rubbing them away.

"How am I being a jackass?" I asked, going for nonchalant even though I needed to blow off some steam with either a fist to a face or a fist around my cock.

"You're scaring all my friends away."

"Since when is that jock from the football team your friend?"

"Well, he's a newer friend," she reasoned with a saucy tilt of her chin.

"Uh huh. He scared off easily enough, but he's not the one I really want gone for good."

"Devon?"

I glanced over at her, her narrowed gaze making my chub swell to full-on ready to fuck. Rather than reply, I returned my attention to the road.

"He's going to be my sweet sixteen, you know."

A muscle in my jaw ticked.

"I've been saving my first kiss for him, on my birthday."

Not if I stole it first…

I forced my tensed body to relax, my mind spinning like a motherfucker. Knowing her, even though she definitely wanted my mouth on hers, she would cry foul.

Too young, I reminded myself, my jaw aching from grinding my teeth.

She didn't speak again, and I left her to her silence, wondering not for the first time how I could get under her skin and poke, prod.

Should have gotten all up in Jenny's ass every second I could, but the wedding day smile had fucking wrecked my ability to focus on the plans I'd made to ruin Addilyn's life.

I followed her ass up the winding staircase, wishing I could bury my face between her asscheeks less than five feet from my face, swishing back and forth with every step upward. Crowding a bit too close earned me a hiss over her shoulder, and damn if my dick didn't leak in my jeans.

"What?" I asked with a smirk, so goddamn in love with making her angry, I wanted to laugh.

She narrowed her eyes and jerked back around, finding the landing.

I stayed on her ass all the way to her bedroom door.

"Do you mind?" she growled the words over her shoulder at me.

"Not at all," I said, inches away from her backside.

She grabbed the door's handle, and I reached past her to close my fist atop hers.

"Let me pull that stick out of your ass," I whispered against her ear, ready to beg.

Her gulp, the shudder that made her body shiver over my front caused my dick to strain, and I bit back a groan.

"You smell like a fresh peach—and I'm so goddamn hungry, princess." A lick over the shell of her ear earned me a barely-there headbutt to the nose, and I grunted, whipping my head back but pushing her full on against the closed door.

Face to the side and cheek on the oak panel, she parted her lips, her eyelashes fluttering shut.

I eyed the corner of her mouth.

Pressed my dick along the top curve of her ass,

lower lip between my teeth to keep from moving my hips and grinding against her.

"Don't," she whispered, her breath sweet like cherries—Swedish Fish.

"Don't what?" I asked, swiping my thumb over my nose to check for blood from her attempted headbutt.

"Don't take what isn't yours."

"That first kiss?" I asked, lowering my face once more, a goddamn breath away from her lips.

We both panted, and every muscle in my body screamed to let loose on her. Her sweet peach scent swarmed my nose, spun my goddamn brain.

"Please," my princess whispered, "don't."

I hesitated, so fucking tempted, but swallowing against the rage to ravish, I pulled away. Pushing distance between us that fucking zinged with lust whether she wanted to admit to it or not didn't come easy, but I managed.

"One day, princess," I muttered, my voice strained, "you're going to be begging me for the opposite."

"In your dreams," she spat and slipped into her room, slamming the door so damn fast, I didn't have time to blink.

"Daytime fantasies too," I hollered so she'd hear the truth of what she did to me.

Perhaps I wouldn't be so quick to head south come graduation.

I ambled down the hallway toward my bedroom, chuckling as my bathroom door slammed and clicked from the inside.

She could lock me out of both her bedroom and her mind, but for how long?

And would sticking around be worth the aggravation of living under the same roof as Dad?

I considered the idea until the next morning when she stomped down the stairs, ready for school. "You so much as touch me, and I swear to fucking God, Gideon Destil, I'll tell your father. I'll tell the sheriff—and you'll end up in jail while his son and I take all of each other's firsts!" Fire blazed in her eyes, giving me yet another chub. "Mess with me and I'll ruin you!"

A flounce of her hair and the little bitch let herself out the door, leaving me laughing after her.

Goddamn, did she get me going, but I guessed I wouldn't be touching until after her birthday.

That didn't mean I had to sit back and let Devon have that first kiss once she was no longer jailbait though.

13

Addilyn

Gideon against my back, feeling how hard I made him, how badly he wanted me, had shaken me up to the point I hadn't even gone downstairs the rest of the night. I didn't call Jenny either. What could I tell her that wouldn't have her swooning and calling me an idiot for not taking advantage of the empty house and a horny man who wanted to lay claim to every inch of my body?

I had the tremors so damn bad I couldn't even get my homework done. At least I'd managed to get dinner by ringing the phone down in the kitchen so the housekeeper on duty could bring me a sandwich.

Plugging up my ears had kept me from hearing Gideon's nightly masturbation session later once I heard the shower running, but I still imagined it behind my clenched eyelids.

And feeling his gaze latch onto me when I came

down the stairs in the morning...well. My insides swirled with arousal I shouldn't have, desire that pissed me off. My stepbrother needed to be put into place, so I decided to do just that even though my stomach fluttered and the devil on my shoulder begged me to let go of my stubbornness and give in already.

The threat of the sheriff seemed to do the trick.

I felt Gideon's stare all through school, that electrical charge whenever he came into sight, but at least he kept his distance.

By sixth period, Jenny expected something was up and cornered me against my locker while we switched out books for our last class. "What the hell is going on?" she hissed, frowning. "What happened with you two?"

My skin tingled, alerting me to Gideon in close proximity, and I knew who Jenny looked at when she glanced up the hallway. Why try to keep anything from her? She could read me easier than anyone.

"He backed me against my bedroom door last night—"

"Oh shit!" Her eyes grew round.

"And was an inch away from kissing me," I whispered, "and I told him not to."

She groaned, clutched her books to her chest, and tipped her head back. "You idiot!"

Exactly as I'd expected.

"How could you say no? Are you crazy? And why didn't you call me last night to give me all the juicy details?"

I shrugged, because I wasn't sure how to tell her I hadn't wanted to talk about it. Dissect the way he made me feel. "I was too shaken up," I went with. "As for saying no, I'm going to have that sweet sixteen kiss, Jenny. And it belongs to Devon. He knows it, I know it—hell, we talked about it in fifth grade when he tried to steal a kiss and I smacked him. Remember?"

"Yeah." She blew out an exhale.

"We pinky swore to be each other's first kiss, and I keep my promises."

"Even when a fine piece of man like your brother jerks off every night thinking about you?"

"Step," I muttered a reminder, slamming my locker door shut harder than necessary.

"Who gives a fuck," she muttered back, falling in beside me as I strode away from the feel of the jackass's stare on my backside. "You seriously need to take advantage of that shit before he decides he wants someone else and you're left wishing you had."

Devon approached, his smile and goofy lope easing my frown and bringing on a small case of butterflies like always. I wished in that moment he made my whole body break out in goosebumps and cold sweats like Gideon did. With a wink, Devon passed us by, and I told myself waiting for that day in March, for him to fulfill his promise, would be worth it.

If only I could convince the part of my brain that had fallen down the rabbit hole of incognito tab Googling.

"So did you tell your mother you don't want to do that brunch for your birthday?"

Yet another shitty thing to think on.

"No. We just discussed it that one time over breakfast, and she's been too caught up in the wedding and vacation since."

"I think you need to put your foot down for once. It's your birthday—it should be about you, not her."

"When has anything in my life been about me and not her?"

Jenny bumped her shoulder against mine. "Seriously. What the hell is her problem?"

"She married up and got to live a life she'd only dreamed about, but I guess when I came along, she lost most of her newfound independence." I shrugged, having come to terms with the fact that I had an emotionally selfish mother. My throat still tightened regardless.

My best friend clasped my hand. "Well, I for one am beyond happy that she gave birth to you. I can't imagine going through life without my BFF."

Her words lightened the heaviness on my shoulders, and I squeezed her hand. "Same. And nothing will ever come between us. We'll always be close, and our kids will grow up together and love each other just as much as we do."

"Promise?"

"Definitely."

"Good," Jenny stated. "Because you're the only friend I know who keeps her promises."

"You do too," I reminded her, and she blew me a kiss.

Mr. Destil—Lloyd, he insisted I call him once they'd married—returned with my mother after the two weeks I had to walk on eggshells, sneak around the house, and plug my ears on a nightly basis. I managed to avoid Gideon for the most part, staying over at Jenny's more often than not, but even though he continued to give me the kind of looks that set my nerve endings on fire and made my underarms tingle, he kept his distance.

Days passed without incident, and I eventually breathed easier.

Gideon's dad and my mother continued to be wrapped up in one another, half the time not even acknowledging our presence. At least we settled into a quieter routine—until Mother remembered I had a big birthday coming up in early March.

She brought it up one Sunday morning while we sat down to eat breakfast as a family, her new requirement to pretend at being a Normal Rockwell painting.

"Lloyd, darling," she said while smiling at me, zero trace of actual happiness in her cool eyes, "our daughter's sixteenth birthday is next month."

"The big sixteen." Lloyd grinned, and I ignored his light chuckle while nibbling on my toast. "Will it be a sweet one?" His voice hinted at teasing.

Mother actually hissed an admonishment at him I'd heard dozens of times. "Of course it is," Mother stated, her tone haughty. "Addilyn has been brought up as a proper young lady. Isn't that right?"

"Yes, ma'am," I answered on autopilot, wondering not for the first time if she'd sheltered me from boys because she hadn't been.

"And since we're having a girls-only brunch over at the club," Mother continued, "there will be no boys around to steal her first kiss, which she's been saving for that special someone since the first time we discussed waiting."

Gideon slid his foot along mine, and I shot him a glare. The corner of his lips quirked, his eyes promising he'd love to be the one, but I narrowed my eyes, reminding him he'd get no such thing.

"Actually, Mother," I turned toward her, forcing the tension from my face, "I was thinking it would be nice to have the party here. That way Lloyd and Gideon can enjoy the day too."

Bullshit. I just needed a chance to see Devon on

March twelfth, and with Lloyd and his father becoming friends, getting his entire family invited wouldn't be an issue.

"I'm all for cake and ice cream," Lloyd said. "And I'd hate to miss her big day."

"And leave me with a mess to deal with afterward?" Mother shook her head, lips pursed. "I think not. The party will be at the club, and luckily, your birthday is on a Saturday this year. We couldn't have asked for a better day of the week."

I went back to my toast, wishing I had the nerve to remind her that she wouldn't have a mess to clean up. That was what the household staff was for.

Mother went on naming her guest list ideas I tuned out, and Gideon gently touched my foot again with his.

Weary, I didn't bother with a glare. The lust vanished from his eyes, and the empathy crossing the table between us filled me with a similar connection I'd felt on our parents' wedding day.

A rare moment without fighting. An even rarer moment of letting my guard down and allowing whatever it was I felt between us to open up. Expand and leave me breathless.

He knew my pain, witnessed Mother's wrath firsthand—and wanted to protect me from it.

Throat tight, I couldn't swallow my chewed-up toast. I carefully reached for my water to wash it down, remembering the sting of Mother's words after I'd ruined her wedding dress. She'd gone on and on about it after we'd both changed and ended up downstairs at the same time—not intentionally. I'd never been so berated in my life and had found myself flinching beneath her accusations that I'd wanted to steal her happiness on her day.

As if my birth alone hadn't already robbed her of her life's joy.

If only Lloyd had shown up to ease her anger like he'd promised to do. At least I'd managed to escape before her voice escalated to shrieking so everyone in the household would've heard.

I wouldn't have been able to stomach the embarrassment.

Her new husband must have worked his magic once they had retired for the night because Mother had handed over my cell while walking out the door for their honeymoon.

"Later today, we can get online to pick out invitations," Mother said, and I opened my mouth to begrudgingly agree, but Gideon beat me to it.

"Actually," he said, setting his utensils upside down on his empty plate, "Addilyn and I are going on a sightseeing tour this afternoon."

I stared at him, face and mind blank. We had no such plans—but did he lie because he felt bad for me or because he wanted to get me alone? Clearing my throat, I nodded. It didn't matter. The thought of spending hours poring over invitations—because that's what she'd made me do with her for my birthday party the year before—churned my stomach.

"Yeah," I agreed, holding his gaze. "We'll be gone most of the day."

He grinned, dimples and all, even though his eyes narrowed a bit with a knowing look.

Guess he planned to get me alone. Great. Still, better than spending time with Mother.

"I'm glad to hear the two of you are going on an outing together. I swear you fight like cats and dogs without all the hissing and barking," Mother stated with a fake laugh.

I wiped my mouth with my linen napkin and glanced at Lloyd. He winked at me.

"May we be excused, Mother?" I asked, not needing to force a smile that came easily from his calming presence.

"Of course, sweetheart." She waved us away, her painted lips tilting up. "Enjoy yourselves!"

"She's just happy to have the house to themselves," I whispered to Gideon once the dining room door shut behind us. "What'd you really have in mind?" I asked, hands on my hips while spinning to face him.

He took his time glancing down over my blouse and dark jeans—a semi decent outfit for breakfast in Mother's eyes. "Let's go fly the friendly skies," he said, returning his focus to my face.

At least he hadn't claimed to want to steal me away, steal a kiss *from* me like I'd expected him to.

"And I suppose I'll be paying since you never have a single dollar on you," I said even though I knew from his own mouth his dad didn't have any money.

"Dutch, sure."

"It's not a date," I snipped and spun on my heel.

He followed along like he always did, probably checking out my ass. Warmth flushed through me, but I scowled the rising goosebumps away. "Father took me on a tour over the glaciers when I was four," I told him as I stepped onto the landing. "I barely remember it, really, so I'd love to go again if you're up for it."

"I'm always up for it, princess."

I rolled my eyes. "Gideon."

"Give them a call," Gideon said with a chuckle, heading toward his door rather than mine to box me in again. "See what they have available today."

A shudder rippled over me at the memory of his muscles and heat pressing against my backside. "Hey."

He pulled up short, the door handle in his grasp, one eyebrow raised in question.

So damn fine.

"Thanks."

He nodded, knowing exactly what I spoke of, and disappeared into his bedroom.

———————————

14

Gideon

———————————

The tour Addilyn had taken as a kid wasn't available, so we ended up in a helicopter on her mom's dime. Spoiled princess had a credit card at age fifteen. To be so damn lucky.

I'd given her space while driving south and kept things cool between us, but once we climbed into the helicopter, we sat side by side, our thighs pressed tight. The scent of peaches filled my nose and chubbed me right the fuck up.

Talking to myself the entire damn flight kept my dick in check, but every shift of her body while she peered out the windows—and goddamn her for leaning over me once to get the view I had—made my jaw ache.

I needed to blow a load like a motherfucker.

"Problems?" Addilyn asked all sweetness as I

adjusted myself after settling into the Cherokee for the drive home.

"Yeah," I didn't bother lying.

She snickered. Fucking laughed.

"You think it's funny I've got a boner for you?"

"Actually, it's sick," she sassed back, tossing her ponytail over her shoulder. "We're siblings."

"Step," I bit out and put the car into drive, "and don't pretend being all trapped up inside that helicopter, our thighs brushing each other's, didn't make your panties wet. You're just as twisted and sick as me, princess."

"I'm not aroused by you," she stated, primly placing her hands on her lap.

"You're full of shit. Your nipples, the pulse in your neck, the way you panted when I had you trapped against your bedroom door and almost stole that kiss…don't lie to yourself. You want me."

"Jackass," she muttered.

"Admit it. I turn you on just like you turn me on. It's called chemistry, Addilyn, and there's nothing sick about it."

She didn't reply, and I glanced over while heading north up the highway to find pink staining her cheeks.

"Yeah." I faced forward, grinning. "You're wet."

"Change of subject, please," she hissed but remained all prissy-like in her seat.

"Okay." I toyed with a few ideas, enjoying her

tone even though my balls ached for her to wrap her lips around them one at a time and suck them into her warm, wet mouth. "Do you ever touch yourself when you hear me jacking off in the shower?"

"Gideon!"

Fuck, did she sound like her mom. My dick cringed, same as my facial muscles. "Answer the question."

"I'll do no such thing."

"Aaaaand, that would be a yes. You really *aren't* so pure like your mother claims, are you?" I grinned, needing to adjust myself again which earned me another hiss from her plump lips.

"God, Gideon, can you please keep from touching your…penis when I'm around you?"

"Nope." I popped the P. "You make me hard. My jeans choke the fuck out of my dick, and since you won't give me relief, I gotta get myself comfortable until I have a chance to rub one out later."

"Oh. My. God," she muttered, shifting on her seat to angle her attention out the passenger window.

"So, are you aroused or wanting to escape right now?" I tossed out, glancing her way.

She shot me another glare that caused my hard length to jerk, bent out of shape in its prison. "I should've stayed home."

"And be burdened with required sit-down Mother time?" I snorted a sarcastic laugh. "Please. She's a goddamn raving lunatic, and you'd rather be here with me, loving our banter, eating up how I make you shiver and pant."

"I don't love anything about you, Gideon Destil," she claimed, chin lifting as she crossed her arms beneath her tits, making my teeth tingle for a taste of her neck. "I'd go so far as to say I lean toward *hate* when it comes to you."

"Feeling's mutual," I lied to the snob needing to be brought down a notch or two, my smile fading. "But that doesn't mean I wouldn't lick and bite every inch of your tight body given the chance."

"If you ever touch me, you'll find out exactly how much I hate you. Remember who my friends are."

I didn't bother telling her she was more than welcome to touch *me* whenever the fuck she wanted.

I'd had enough banter with her prissy ass for the day. My goddamn balls couldn't handle another round, so I let her sit in quiet the rest of the ride home.

***

"Gideon," Dad called and waved me toward his office. He stood on the threshold like he'd been waiting for me to come down the stairs.

I had finished up my homework and planned to hit the weights in the finished basement Ingrid had bought for the two of us. Goddamn cunt—I hated her more than I hated my own father, but at least she knew how to butter a guy up. I forced those special smiles for her whenever she spent money on me. Fucking bitch deserved that at least, and it always made it easier for her to buy me more shit too.

"What's up?" I asked, following Dad into the office that had belonged to his wife's old husband she'd offered him use of.

Dad nodded toward a chair facing his deck, and I lowered myself into it, my shoulders tensing and breaths growing shallow. He didn't appear angry—no scowl or dented brow—but Dad never asked to speak to me in private unless something was wrong.

Maybe Ingrid had finally gotten under his skin and he was ready to call it quits.

Fuck—that thought sucked balls. I hated Alaska, but I needed more time to get under Addilyn's skin. Show her she wasn't all that, bring her down to my level—

"Grades good?" Dad settled into his chair and shuffled a few things around on his desk.

"Yes." I didn't bother with a "sir" like Ingrid would require when in her presence.

"Making any friends?"

"None that will get me to stay here after graduation if that's what you're wondering."

"I'm actually coming to enjoy Alaska."

So much for him calling it quits and heading back home.

"I'll be out of your hair come June because there's

no way in hell I'm staying up here in this damn ice box."

Lips pursing, he finally turned his focus on me. "I was talking to Sheriff Bradshaw at the dinner Ingrid and I went to last weekend."

Fucking lovely. I waited rather than saying anything.

"It seems as though Devon feels animosity from you."

As well the fucker should. "He sniffs after Addilyn's ass like he wants a bite." I went with what I expected Dad would hate to get him to understand my need to protect her—only from everyone but myself.

Sure enough, a muscle twitched in his jaw. "Given the chance, would he attempt anything, do you think?"

"Looking after the princess's innocence?" I asked, keeping my tone light, without a trace of suggestion.

"According to her mother, Addilyn is pure, and yes, I'd like to keep her that way until she's ready for a man in her life."

My stomach clenched up tight as fuck as I studied his face.

He held my stare, his cold and closed off, but he couldn't get shit past me.

Grooming, I'd heard it called. Well, attempts, anyway. I didn't think he'd broken through Addilyn's walls enough to get her ready for his attention. Dad wouldn't ever earn her trust. My princess was too smart—same as she wouldn't trust me.

I'm sick, just like him.

I lost our stare down and glanced out the window to my right, the afternoon's dark sky settling over me like a heavy weight.

"I want you to stay the hell away from Devon, Gideon. Addilyn isn't yours to protect."

"She's my sister," I barely held back the snip in my tone.

"She's not blood and not your concern."

I got the hint, the true meaning behind his words that had nothing to do with Devon Bradshaw. Dad would take what he wanted, and I would sit back and let it happen—because I owed him one.

"She hates me anyway," I stated, straightening my shoulders in attempt to pass myself off as confident, uncaring of his veiled threat.

"I'm putting a security system in the house."

I blinked at his one-eighty in topics but waited.

"She'll be sixteen in a couple weeks. Legal. I expect young men will start taking an interest."

They already had, but I didn't bother telling him. Last thing Addilyn needed was my father to decide to up his plans for her before some other punk got to her first. "What kind of system are you talking?"

"Cameras. Inside and outside the entire property."

Fucker. I knew exactly why he wanted cameras everywhere.

I forced a grin. "Just not in our shared bathroom," I said with a laugh. "My bedroom, either. I won't be able to jerk off knowing you might accidentally get an eyeful of my dick and balls."

Dad chuckled like we shared some sort of male camaraderie shit. "Can't have that."

Yeah, I wanted to tell him. *Can't have her for as long as I'm around either.*

15

Addilyn

Lloyd and Mother had cameras installed throughout the house—minus bathrooms and bedrooms, but the idea of someone watching me walking the hallways creeped me out. I didn't bother talking to Mother privately though. Her whole "keep my sweetheart pure as long as possible" speech would have been spewed yet again.

Not that I was allowed to have boys over, anyway. What'd they expect? Devon to come tossing pebbles at my bedroom window? He would never do something like that, but even if he did, I wouldn't let him in. Yes, I wanted—promised—him my first kiss, but I wasn't interested in *that*.

Not yet, anyway.

Maybe someday, a young man who wasn't Gideon would make me crave the same way he did, and I'd be ready to give in. Until then, I would ignore my stepbrother and hide away until he got the point.

Hanging out in my bedroom became my favorite pastime, and I locked myself in from after school for homework and Chit'n Chat time until dinner when I had no choice but to sit as a family.

Every. Damn. Night.

Mother texted me less than ten minutes after I'd gotten home from school.

Mother: **Come to the parlor, please. I'm finalizing plans for your party.**

"Just great." Huffing a groan, I shot back a **Yes, ma'am** and shut down my laptop, expecting I wouldn't be getting back to my homework until dinner finished since I'd been putting off the required sit-down with her for a couple weeks. At least she had said please for a change.

Feet dragging, I made my way downstairs to her sitting room, feeling as though I walked to my doom.

Garish yellows splashed across the room like an artist's canvas, blindingly bright from all the lights she kept on in attempts to ward off her winter blues. I blinked a few times, adjusting my eyes. She sat behind her desk in the corner.

"Have a seat, sweetheart."

I did as told, folding my hands on my lap.

"I just got off the phone with Paul over at Perfect Pastries," she said in a low voice while scribbling something on a sheet of paper with one of her gel pens—probably in yellow. "He's agreed to make a chocolate, three-tiered cake for your birthday."

Chocolate. Her favorite.

I bit my tongue rather than argue which wouldn't have accomplished a damn thing.

"And I went ahead and also ordered centerpieces since you couldn't be bothered to help in the decision-making."

She hadn't asked for my opinion for them, but whatever. I wasn't in the mood to argue. My ears weren't up to the task of being blasted.

"I decided on white daisies for purity—like you."

That, at least, I couldn't just let go. "They make me sneeze," I told her, keeping my tone neutral even though my insides tightened up.

"Just don't get too close." She snapped the cap back on her pen and turned to face me while I blinked at her. "They're elegant in their simplicity."

"I'm *allergic* to daisies." I couldn't believe I had to remind my own mother of that fact.

"And they're what I prefer," she snipped back, "so just don't go sticking your nose in them."

While I wasn't deathly allergic, she knew they caused my face to splotch up and my nose to run. Did she *want* me to look a mess for my sweet sixteen in retaliation for soaking her gown at the country club? Heat rose inside me like a swelling brush fire, ready to combust and burn everything in its path.

I managed to bite back my snort, but not my tongue. "Seriously?"

"You like what I like," she reasoned which made no damn sense to me.

Since when?

"Name one thing we both enjoy, Mother." I barely held onto the flames searing my insides.

"We have plenty in common." She waved her hand as though there were too many to be named.

"Name. One." Crossing my arms, I stared, waiting, knowing I opened a can of worms that would explode in an array of grime and blood.

But enough already.

Mother eyed me, her own gaze narrowing. "Don't get all short with me, young lady."

"You love spas," I told her. "I hate them. You love chocolate. I've always preferred vanilla. You'll choose a nap over a walk outside every day. You love long hair, and I want mine cut in a bob."

I should've let it rest right there, but the heat flared to flames, and I gave in to the need to finally voice what I felt—what I knew to be true.

"You like to be entertained," I continued on before she could say a word, "have people cater to you while I'd rather *do* things and make my own entertainment. We have nothing in common, Mother. We never have!" My voice raised, and I couldn't stop, my arms starting to flail. "When are you going to open your eyes and see that? When are you going to finally recognize that my life isn't about you?"

Red stained Mother's cheeks. "Everything I've done has been for you," she hissed the second I paused for breath.

Hopping up to my feet, I met her pissy stare, my hands on my hips and my insides quivering. "Bullshit!"

"Addilyn Jane!" Mother stood too, but I wasn't about to back down. The dam had been opened. It was time to let it all out.

She could have my cell phone—unloading would be worth it. She could cancel my birthday party that sounded like an absolute bore anyway.

"Every decision you've ever made about me has been for your benefit," I told her, my low voice shaking while I pulled my cell from my back pocket. "The latest being those men you brought into our home! Do you know what it's like sharing a bathroom? Having to put up with a protective jackass who growls whenever one of my friends gets close to me? This life sucks, Mother, and it's your fault!"

"You jealous, ungrateful bitch," Mother shrieked. "It's *my* time, my turn for happiness!"

"It's always been your time!" I screamed right back, tossing my cell onto the chair I'd hopped up from. "But this party isn't about you! It's my birthday, *my* sweet sixteen. Why can't you just listen to what I want for a change? Hear what I'm saying rather than plan your next words when I talk? You don't hear me. You've *never* heard me! It's like I'm not good enough—I can't ever live up to your high damn expectations!"

"You can forget about your party, young lady!" she screamed, spittle flying from her lips.

Expected, but I couldn't give a single shit. "Good! I don't want what you planned anyway!" Spinning on my heel, I rushed for the door, my insides trembling, hands shaking.

"I don't want to be like her!" Mother shrieked like a damn banshee, totally mental, something glass smashing in the room behind me. "Do you hear what you're doing to me, Addilyn Jane? I swore I would always stay in control, and you're constantly pushing and pushing. All I ever wanted was to escape her—and now I'm *becoming* her!"

Mother's rant followed me out into the hallway, her voice ringing in my ears as I sprinted up the stairs.

Escape her...becoming her...

Had Mother's relationship with her own mom been as horrid as ours was? The thought should have pained my heart, but Mother had crushed me one too many times to stir up any understanding or empathy for what she went through as a child.

She might have become the woman who'd raised her, but no way in hell would I continue down that path.

"Addilyn!" Lloyd called after me, but I ignored him as he strode from his office toward Mother's parlor.

She broke down into screaming hysterics, and tears welled in my own eyes, spilling onto my cheeks as I rushed through the carpeted hallway and into my bedroom.

While the release had felt good, my heart ripped in two over her absolute disregard for me. Even after finally hearing the reason Mother and my grandmother were estranged, I couldn't rouse an ounce of pity for the childhood she must've had.

Too much damage had been done.

I slammed my bedroom door, tossed myself onto my bed like a toddler having a tantrum, and screamed my pity party sobs into my pillow.

It's joked that all teenagers say they hate their life —but I truly did.

Reality as I knew it couldn't get any worse.

16

Gideon

Like a couple of cats, Ingrid and Addilyn went at it, their raised voices and shrieks echoing throughout the entire house. The shouting ended, and I listened from where I sprawled on my bed as footsteps rushed past my bedroom. Addilyn's door slammed seconds later, her sobs reaching me within a heartbeat.

Jaw clenched, I considered going downstairs and telling that bitch Ingrid that every word I'd overheard about her being a selfish woman had been true. Knowing Dad would be consoling her though, I wasn't about to step foot down those damn stairs.

Addilyn on the other hand…

I eyed the bathroom door I'd kept open. On the opposite side, hers wasn't all the way shut.

The thought of the pain she must be feeling

pulled me off my bed, and I quietly pushed her bathroom door wide. "Addilyn?"

She didn't pause in her crying but didn't tell me to fuck off or get lost, so I moved across her room, settling onto the edge of her bed.

"Hey."

"Go away," she muttered into her pillow, sniffing and curling into a ball.

"Come here." I pulled her sideways onto my lap and earned a punch and curse, but I squeezed her tight. "Shh. Let me hold you, princess."

She melted. Goddamn gave into the comfort my insides ached to offer. Her tears soaked my T-shirt, her hands grasping at my back like I was her sole source of life, her rock.

Filled me fucking full to bursting—and not my nuts.

The connection I'd felt for her snapped tight inside me again, the rushing need to protect the young woman who'd allowed me another peek inside overriding all other senses. I wanted to make her smile with the light that could warm a man through. I wanted to soothe away her heartache. I wanted to carry her burdens.

Give her every fucking part of my soul.

Scared the living shit outta me. I was supposed to hate her, blame her for being responsible for my uprooted life and making me feel less than her rich ass.

But I couldn't.

I soaked in the warmth of her, the sweet scent of her. Clung to the idea that I could be the one she ran to whenever she hurt and wanted someone to help shoulder whatever bothered her.

As soon as her tears lessened, I tightened my hold so she would attempt escape. Couldn't let her go just yet.

"I remember my grandfather," I murmured, closing my eyes and seeing the memory of the gray-haired man my father looked like. "He was a drunk. Gambler. My grandmother wasn't much better. A controlling drunk."

Addilyn quieted and rested silent on my lap, all the encouragement I needed to keep talking, to make her linger in my arms.

"Both are dead now," I told her. "One cancer, the other a heart attack."

"Your mom?" Addilyn whispered, her voice raw and shaky.

"Left us when I was three for some Hollywood producer," I answered without feeling since I could barely recall the woman. "Broke Dad's heart. He became his father." A frown dented my brow. "But at least he went to rehab for the booze."

"That's why he doesn't drink."

"Yeah, but he's the perfect product of both of his parents. He can't control his gambling habit, but he holds tight reins on anything else he can."

Myself included.

"He's a gambler?"

How much to share… Surely her mother knew about my father's broke bank account by now. "Let's just say he doesn't have the money to buy me shit to make up for being such a dick."

"My mother will buy you whatever you ask for—if you stay on her good side," Addilyn said with a sigh. "I still haven't decided if it's her way of showing affection or if she's trying to make me forget she's such a selfish bitch."

I doubted Ingrid attempted to show love she wasn't capable of, but I didn't want to upset the princess any more than she already was.

"Real nice of fate to give us pieces of shit for parents, huh?"

Addilyn let out a heavy sigh, seeming to sink even further into me. "Yeah."

We sat silent for a few minutes, and I filled my lungs with the scent of peaches. So damn soft…

I clenched my teeth, fighting off a boner over having her so close, so…compliant. Sure, her sass got me off, but submissive Addilyn? Fuck yeah.

"Are we doomed to be fucked up, Gideon?" she asked, her voice small. Broken. "Can we escape our genes?"

"I'm nothing like him." *Except for wanting you.* Damn chub. "And I'll never *be* like him," I tacked on for good measure.

"I don't want to become my mother."

"So don't." I shifted Addilyn away from my groin, desperate to keep her in my arms for just a few moments more. Her becoming aware of my thickening dick would end our momentary truce, and I wanted to soak in more of her softness before the hissing cat returned. "Decide you'll be her opposite —which you already are, in my opinion—and you'll convince yourself of that very thing."

Addilyn sat up, her blue eyes bright from tears. The pain in them, the need for understanding, for love, punched me in the gut. Stole the air from my lungs.

My hand shook as I smoothed back her hair. Like silk. Warm.

Damn near perfect.

Dick swollen, I stared at her lips, and she stiffened against the arm I had wrapped around her back.

"Don't," she whispered.

"Don't what?"

"Kiss me."

I couldn't help smirking and stating the truth since our temporary peace had definitely come to an end. "I want to do a hell of a lot more than kiss you, princess, and you want me to. When are you finally going to admit it and give me a little taste? Hmm?"

She shoved against my chest, scrambled to escape me—and fucking kneed me in the nuts.

"Goddamnit!" I groaned, clutching my groin and doubling over.

"Serves you right, jackass," she hissed, hopping off her bed. "Now get the hell out of my bedroom before I holler for your dad."

That would be a problem.

"Give me a second to catch my fucking breath, you bitch!" I gasped between moans, cupping my aching groin. "You kneed me in the goddamn balls!"

"Because you're a sick fuck who shouldn't be saying that stuff to me!"

I rolled off the bed and hobbled toward the bathroom, my eyes watering.

"That's right," she said, following after me to lock me out, probably. "Run back to your room like a dog with its tail between its legs. You know I could ruin you with one word in the sheriff's ear."

Goddamn bitch.

Straightening, I slammed my fist into the wall with a growl—better to dent drywall than break her goddamn nose.

One stride took me over the threshold into the bathroom, and Addilyn slammed her door behind me, the click barely sounding above my curses.

I'd gotten a feel of what it was like to hold Addilyn in my arms, and I knew without doubt I'd crave it until I rested six feet under.

Fucking bitch.

I curled up on my bed, cursing her name and my

aching nuts, but I found comfort in the fact she wasn't miserable over her mother anymore. I'd rather her be spitting angry at me than crying over that cunt.

17

Addilyn

I refused to attend dinner, not that I even knew if our so-called family sat down to one.

Lloyd came knocking at my door around bedtime, but I told him I didn't want to talk. He left me alone without argument. Gideon didn't knock, not that I'd expected him to, but I wouldn't have spoken with him either.

He showered while I plugged my ears, and eventually the house rested quietly.

The opposite of my mind.

I'd enjoyed being held by my stepbrother way too much. At first, I'd soaked in the warmth, the comfort of a male hug I hadn't had since…I couldn't remember. The memory of my father's arms hadn't carried through the years, and I ended up crying against Gideon more over that fact than the way my mother had hurt me yet again.

But then he had to go and get hard and start spewing sick shit.

Which you actually liked.

"Ugh!" I punched my pillow and curled into a ball, aroused and revulsed at the same time.

Hours passed, but I couldn't sleep. Without a phone, I couldn't call Jenny to unload and at least hear some verbal comfort. Mother didn't allow me a laptop in my room after I finished homework, so communication fell short in that area too.

I had nothing.

No one.

And it sucked big balls. Hairy ones like on that goat Jenny and I had giggles over at the farm we'd visited for a field trip in the fifth grade.

Acid seemed to eat away at my stomach, and a little after one in the morning, I decided to sneak downstairs and get something to help ease the ache. I hadn't eaten since lunch, and between the gut-twisting bullshit with my mother and the unwanted way my body reacted to Gideon and his brutal truth bombs, it was no wonder my stomach complained.

A buttery bagel sounded divine, so that was what I crept around the kitchen for, taking care to make as little noise as possible.

The light flicked on at the same time the toaster popped up my snack, and I let out a muffled shriek around my hand.

Lloyd stood just inside the kitchen in sleep pants and a t-shirt, his dark hair sticking up.

"What are you doing?" I whispered, glancing beyond him. My stomach hardened over the thought Mother might be behind him.

He ambled into the kitchen—without Mother.

"I'm getting a snack," he said, opening the fridge door. "Why are you in the kitchen this late at night?"

"*Sneaking* a snack," I muttered, placing my toasted bagel onto a small plate, my hand still shaking from the adrenaline rush his sudden arrival caused.

He shut the door without retrieving anything and turned to lean against it, arms crossed. "Why sneaking?"

"Because if Mother knew I was down here," I said, buttering my bagel, "she'd have a fit and take my phone for another week."

Lloyd stared at me hard, and even though I expected I sounded like a whining toddler, I didn't have the energy to give a shit.

I slumped at the table and took a big bite. Warm butter oozed, the fresh, delicious bagel filling my mouth and soothing my churning stomach.

"You both said some pretty awful things to each other this afternoon."

Just when I'd thought he might not be so bad…

I went back for another bite of my divine snack, intent on ignoring him.

"But we all say and do things we don't always

mean." He grabbed the bag of bagels and pushed one into the toaster.

A few minutes later, he sat beside me with a jelly-slathered snack of his own. "I'm going to ask your mother if she would be open to seeing a therapist."

I jerked my gaze his way, slowly chewing.

"But telling you is going to be our little secret, okay?" He shoved a huge bite into his mouth.

I nodded and swallowed. "She's going to explode on you when you suggest it."

He smiled around his bagel, not speaking until he finished. "I'm hoping she won't, but if she does, I'm determined to be patient and loving and do what I can to create a happier home for us."

"That might take manipulation on your part," I muttered and stuck the last bite of bagel between my lips.

"All I want is for us to be happy," Lloyd stated quietly. "And I'll climb mountains if that's what it takes."

I got up and washed my plate, knowing the housekeeper would tell Mother if anything was misplaced or sitting where she hadn't put it before leaving for the night.

Lloyd stood too, and I held out my hand for his plate, washing it up for him.

He leaned against the counter beside me and crossed his arms, pulling his t-shirt tight over his chest. "I can't promise I'll get your cell back to you within twenty-four hours like last time you two fought, but I'll do my best."

"Thanks," I whispered.

"Now get back to bed and I'll make sure to erase the video from the house's cameras showing our midnight rendezvous."

Oh shit. I'd forgotten about that.

I paused from leaving the kitchen and turned back toward him, taking two steps to throw my arms around his waist.

Lloyd wasn't so bad after all.

"Go on." He squeezed me tight then tugged on my hair. "Hit the sack. Things will be better in the morning."

Trusting his promise, I headed up the stairs and burrowed beneath my blankets, breathing out a steady, cleansing sigh.

Mother's husband wanted us to be happy, he wanted to help. With how much he loved her, I found a seed of hope to cling to that things might actually get better, exactly as he'd stated.

Sleep came easier.

<hr>

Gideon, thankfully, kept his distance as we all tiptoed around each other the next couple of days.

Good thing, too, seeing as how I dreamed about snuggling against him every. Damn. Night. His lap had offered the kind of strength I'd been missing my whole life. Pulling away had physically hurt my heart, but I didn't trust him. Didn't trust my hormones to not give in to what he always teased me about.

I hadn't meant to bash him with my knee, and the hole he'd left in my bedroom wall?

I felt compelled to move the painting beside it enough to hide the damage his anger had caused—since I'd been the responsible one. Why I wanted to protect him from Mother's wrath, I wasn't sure. Perhaps because he'd held me and given comfort when I'd needed it most. Or perhaps I couldn't stand the thought of anyone else having to deal with her making them feel small and worthless.

She drank more than was healthy, her eyes red beneath all her makeup. Lloyd doted on her, coddling her like a baby while I was left to fend for myself emotionally.

Chin lifted, I feigned a strength I didn't feel. At least Mother didn't confront me over our major altercation. I guess she didn't know how to handle our outburst any more than I did. Anger continued to grip my stomach tight, making eating difficult. I couldn't look at her without my heart getting stabbed all over again.

Lloyd must have suggested she see a therapist a few nights after our little snack time together. Even through their bedroom door, I could make out her raised voice and harsh words over being perfectly fine, thank you very much. She didn't need some head doctor to tell her how to raise her daughter.

Locking myself in the bathroom for a long bath had rid me of their voices, but I noticed Mother began to drink heavily afterward, her eyes glassy and more often than not seeking me out to glare in silent accusation.

Twice in the following two weeks, Gideon and I arrived home from school to find her already returned from work. Smelling of booze. Sprawled in her yellow-everything parlor that did nothing to liven her sallow colored cheeks.

Gideon and I exchanged looks when she slurred her words at dinner time but brushed that shit under the bed.

He'd shared personal things while holding me, giving me a better understanding of both him and his father, but I couldn't be bothered with empathy. I had enough shit on my plate to worry about.

"I've officially cancelled your party," Mother said over breakfast the Monday before my birthday.

I hated that my spoon of Apple Jacks halted halfway to my mouth, but I shoveled the cereal in, nodding. Not that I'd expected any different or cared, I told myself.

"No cake, no candles," Mother continued as though rubbing in the extremely late punishment. "No singing, either."

Gideon's jaw clenched, but he made no argument, same as I kept my mouth shut while we finished eating. Mother gave a humph—probably annoyed that cancelling my birthday hadn't seemed to hurt me, but I ignored her.

Lloyd offered a gaze of pity as I hopped up to finish getting ready for school, but I didn't have the energy to return his small smile.

I wouldn't get my sweet sixteen, one of the few things I'd looked forward to in life. I'd been holding out on that kiss for nothing.

"You okay?" Gideon asked as we climbed into his car for the drive to school a few minutes later, both of us in sweatshirts rather than winter coats.

"Yep." I popped the P and pulled out my cell that had finally gotten returned to me before slipping out the door. Lloyd had tried to get it back quickly, and he'd whispered an apology when handing it over, but he hadn't been able to sway her.

Me: **She cancelled my party.**

BFF: **Bitch!**

Me: **Right?**

BFF: **So now what?**

Me: **Don't know, don't care. I just want to fall asleep and not wake up for a few months.**

"Want to talk about it?" Gideon asked as my fingers flew over my screen while texting Jenny.

"Nope."

"Thanks for hanging that picture over the hole in

your wall instead of ratting me out."

I faced him, my gaze narrowing. "When did you go into my room?"

"You left the door cracked open the other day," he said, not making eye contact. "I saw the picture right there."

My eyes narrowed further—I didn't believe a word he said. "Snooping around for another pair of my dirty underwear?"

"Shit." He grinned and shifted like he was getting a hard-on. "Jerking off just isn't the same without the scent of you and that silk wrapped around my dick."

"Sick fuck."

"You know you want it."

"Fuck off, Gideon."

He chuckled, and I turned away with a sniff, lifting my nose into the air so he would see he couldn't affect me.

When I stomped up the school's stairs, Jenny's eyes went wide the second she saw my face. I'd rushed across the parking lot and left Gideon in the dust. "What the hell?"

Guess I still looked mad enough to fight a grizzly. "It's not that big of a deal," I stated about the party being cancelled rather than telling her what Gideon had said in his car.

Devon held the door for us to go inside the school, smiling at me as usual.

"What's wrong?" he asked, falling into step on my other side.

"My mother cancelled my birthday party," I told him. "Long story—don't ask."

"That sucks."

"Yeah." I tried for a smile that totally wobbled.

"You still want that sweet sixteen kiss?" he asked me, his goofy grin prompting a real one to turn up my lips.

"Of course."

"Then I'll just have to throw a party Saturday night because I've been looking forward to that day for half my life."

"Her mom will never let her go," Jenny said with a laugh from my other side.

"So, she can say she's sleeping over at your house, and the two of you can sneak out," Devon said with a shrug.

I considered his suggestion while opening my locker and unloading my backpack. Jenny did the same as me, but Devon lingered as though waiting for an answer while dozens of kids rushed past toward their homerooms.

"I'm always up for a sleepover," Jenny said, shoving her coat into her locker. "We can hang at my house, tell my parents we're going to watch a movie in my room, then lock ourselves away. There are no cameras at our place, so sneaking out my bedroom window and across the yard won't be a problem."

"And how do you suggest we get to Devon's?" I asked with more snark than she deserved. "Sure, it's warming up a bit outside, but while I love walking, two miles in the dark? No thanks."

"I'll have my older brother drive over to pick you up."

I shut my locker and turned to face Devon. Guess he wanted that kiss pretty badly if he offered the older brother he couldn't stand. "You'd really ask him to do that for me?"

"Addilyn, there isn't much I wouldn't do for you." His goofy, adoring grin returned.

One of my best friends, the guy who'd begged me to be his girlfriend since grade school, was going to give me my birthday wish.

I nodded, feeling lighter than I had in weeks. Months.

"Okay." I glanced at Jenny. "Okay. It's a plan. We're going to lie and sneak out like real teenagers."

"That's my girl." Devon bumped my elbow and scurried away.

"I'm not your girl," I muttered to myself.

"That boy is so far gone on you."

I snorted at Jenny, both of us turning toward our homeroom. "Since the second grade when I tripped him by accident while playing tag."

"He scraped up his knee," Jenny said.

"And laying there on the ground he told me—"

"—I think I like you," we both said at the same time and laughed.

Poor guy. I was half tempted to agree to be his girlfriend just for being so faithful. Devon. The one guy friend I had and the only person besides Jenny I could count on.

A shiver slid down my spine, and I glanced over my shoulder while walking into class.

Gideon studied me from where he stood by his locker.

I lifted my chin and turned away, refusing to admit to myself I could count on him too.

I waited until Thursday night after dinner to attempt to set my plan into place. Mother had two glasses of wine with her meal and a third settled in her hand as she and Lloyd headed to the parlor. She'd smiled a few times at dinner while speaking with her doting husband, and I thought I might stand a chance of getting her to agree.

The birthday hadn't been a topic of conversation in three days, and with all the sudden drinking, maybe she'd forgotten what day Saturday was to me.

"Oh, I wanted to ask if I could sleep over at Jenny's on Saturday," I said, stopping at the stairs leading to the second floor, one foot on the bottom riser.

Mother and Lloyd paused in their walk to the parlor, both glancing my way.

"We're going to watch our favorite movie and eat a bunch of popcorn and Swedish Fish."

Lloyd's gaze seared my face, but I kept my focus on Mother who weaved a bit, leaning on him. Guess she'd had a glass or two prior to dinner too.

"Didn't we have dinner plans for Saturday anyway, darling?" Lloyd asked mother, squeezing her tight against his side. "I'm sure it would be okay for our sweetheart to go."

The guy *really* wasn't so bad after all.

"That's fine," Mother said, waving her free hand as though she couldn't be bothered with me.

He shot me a quick wink, and I mouthed a 'thank you' as he kept his smiling eyes on me while steering her around toward the parlor.

I offered him his first grin and sailed up the stairs. Once I disappeared from sight, I let my excitement out, breathless giggles bursting from me.

"She said yes," I holler-whispered into my cell the second Jenny answered my call.

"Oh my god! I was sure she'd make you stay home."

"She's so damn drunk, she probably doesn't even know what day it is."

Jenny laughed.

"Now to figure out how to get me over there," I said, sprawling onto my back on my bed.

"I already asked my mom if we could pick you up."

"Sweet!" I laughed again, that light feeling of having things go my way for once filling my chest. "You're sure they won't check on us after we lock ourselves in your room?"

"I'm sure. You know how much they trust me."

"Yeah," I agreed, "and it's well-earned. You're one of the few people *I* trust."

"Who else?"

"Devon," I didn't hesitate to answer. I considered naming Lloyd too but decided to keep that bit to myself, considering how much I'd claimed to hate him and his son. "Can you believe he's willing to throw a party for me? I mean, what a sweetheart!"

"He just wants that kiss," Jenny said with a snort.

"Well, he's definitely getting that kiss Saturday night," I stated, butterflies dancing in my belly. "He deserves it for going out of his way to make my birthday special."

We chatted a bit more and made plans on what to wear, knowing Devon's dad would have a big bonfire outside like he usually did whenever they allowed him to have friends over. Hardly any snow had dumped on us since early February, and the warmer weather had pretty much melted all the white except for plowed piles here and there.

Spring seemed to have arrived early—and I finally had something to look forward to again.

18

Gideon

So, the girls planned on sneaking over to Devon's. I'd overheard enough of their phone conversation to figure that shit out.

Devon was throwing a party on Saturday night.

Dad and Ingrid had dinner plans.

That left me with nothing to do but stalk after Addilyn without her knowing. Keep that prick Devon away from her. Talk her into giving *me* her first kiss. Hell, I could've taken it from her that day I held her in my arms. I deserved to be the one to taste her lips for the first time after showing so much damn restraint.

So, I had to get myself an invitation to the party. Slim chance in hell, but better than just showing up and being told to leave by the prick sheriff.

I told myself I could play it cool—so I tried

Friday morning, offering Devon a nod as he held the door open for the girls like he always did.

He split from the girls at their lockers, and I hurried after him. "Heard you're throwing a party," I said, coming up alongside him.

"Yeah."

"Are big brothers invited?"

He snorted and raised his eyebrows while glancing at me, not slowing his quick stride down the hallway. "And why would I ask you to step foot on our property?"

"Because I'm not that bad of a guy, and if you're lucky enough to talk my sis into being your girl, then don't you think we should repair the broken bridge between us?"

He laughed while heading into his homeroom. "See ya 'round, Gid."

Fuck. Lips pressed tight, I sprinted in the opposite direction—and stepped over my homeroom's threshold a second after the bell rang.

My teacher gave me the stink eye, but a flash of my dimples had her nodding toward my assigned seat.

That luck came to a screeching halt just before sixth period when I saw Devon hovering over my princess. Cheeks pink, she peered at him through her lashes, her lips moving, the words lost under the voices of dozens of kids filing through the hallway.

I started their way—and the fucker pushed her hair off her forehead like I'd done.

He fucking touched her with lingering fingertips, and I saw vivid red unlike any jealousy I'd ever felt before.

My stalking toward them couldn't be hindered and went unnoticed by the two fucking love birds.

"Fuck off, Devon," I told him, giving his shoulder a shove the second I got close enough. He slammed against the locker beside her, glaring at me like he had balls to spare.

"Lay off, Gid."

Fucking Gid. Hated that goddamn nickname.

The hallway grew silent, and a crowd gathered, holding their collective breath as though waiting for a showdown that had been brewing since I'd stepped foot into their school.

Devon smiled at my princess right then like I didn't exist and hadn't nearly dislocated his shoulder. Eyes only for her with stars in his own.

My teeth grated, and my hands fisted at my sides. Blood rage swept through me, the same sort that had gotten me thrown into juvie back in California. I wanted to smash his face in, send a river of red over his face.

I slowly counted to calm myself the fuck down. Getting in trouble with the little shit in front of me would leave my princess vulnerable.

Couldn't have that.

"So, I'll see you tomorrow night?" he asked her.

Fuck, he pissed me off.

"Touch Addilyn again," I hissed before she could answer, crowding in close enough he pressed his back against the wall of lockers, "and I'll fucking kill you."

"You can't threaten him like that, Gideon!" Addilyn backhanded my arm. "Leave him alone!"

"See you tomorrow?" Devon asked again while peering around me, ignoring me like I wasn't all up in his face. Ballsy bastard.

"Of course," Addilyn agreed.

"Best heed my warning," I said, my finger in his face. I wanted to rip his goddamn eyes out.

Devon finally met my glare, holding it in unmoved complacency.

He wouldn't throw a first punch, so what could I do but step back?

"I mean it, Devon. One hair on her head, and I'll make you curse your mother for bringing you into this world."

He hesitated but decided to continue on, sauntering off like he owned the goddamn school. With the crowd breaking up around us, I turned back to Addilyn.

"Fuck off, Gideon," she grumbled at me as I hovered the same way Devon had. She grabbed a book and binder out of her locker, shoved another inside, and slammed the door. Those big blue eyes of hers looked my way, and pink fused her cheeks. "Don't you have anything better to do than lurk like an unwanted shadow tossing out death threats?" She snipped, that chin of hers lifting and tempting my hands to hold it. Feel the throb of her pulse. Squeeze until her lips parted.

My dick twitched.

"Lifting your chin like that leaves your neck vulnerable, princess, and to answer your question, nope. There's nothing bullshit about my *promises*. He touches you, he dies."

Smart girl lowered her head a bit as though afraid I might bite the tender flesh beneath her ear like I wanted to. "I told you, he's going to be my first kiss—and I'm getting it tomorrow night whether you like that fact or not, Gideon Destil."

I growled like a goddamn dog, showing my teeth. Ever since I'd held her and she'd cried, soaking my shirt with her tears, all thoughts of anyone else but me putting their hands on her brought out my inner caveman. She made me fucking nuts—like an animal operating on instinct, wanting to take without asking.

But I wasn't my dad.

Addilyn rolled her eyes. "Whatever. Can't you just leave me alone?"

"You'll thank me some day," I stated through gritted teeth, goddamn hard up to change our unfair, fucked situation.

"Doubtful." She waved her hand at the sea of bodies around us. "Why don't you go out? Make friends finally. Find a girlfriend or two."

"Not interested."

"Why not? Every girl in this school, teachers too from what I hear, wants you. Easy pickings to get your…your dick wet," she said, her voice going all soft at the end.

I held her steady gaze, a smirk lifting my lips. "Not interested, princess."

Not in them, anyway.

She shivered and clutched her books to her tits. "You're a creep, you know that?"

"Yep."

"Why are you always up my butt, huh? Why can't you ignore me here like you do at home?"

Up. Her. Butt.

Fuck.

I couldn't find the fucking words to toss back, and she walked away with a huff, leaving me with a boner that required a pit stop at the bathroom which made me late for class.

Without an invitation and expecting I'd be sheriff-escorted off the property if I showed up at Devon's, I decided to throw a wrench in her and Jenny's plans instead.

Dinner Friday night.

The four of us sat there, Ingrid well on her way to being blitzed again, which Dad did nothing about.

He, of all people, knew the path Ingrid travelled. But maybe he wanted her to drink herself to death.

It would save him the problem of getting rid of the burdensome cunt once he decided he'd had enough.

"I heard your boyfriend is throwing a party tomorrow night," I said across the table to Addilyn in a moment's lull between our parent's conversation.

"What's that?" Ingrid asked, her words slurred.

"That Devon boy—Sheriff's kid," I said, watching the princess's attempt to keep her face passive. She fucking seethed beneath her calm exterior. "He's throwing a bonfire party at his parents' place tomorrow. Their whole class is invited."

"Well, Addilyn won't be going. She's having a sleepover at Jenny's," Ingrid attempted to claim in a stately, poised manor. Fucking drunk-assed bitch.

A corner of my lip curled, and I raised an eyebrow, daring Addilyn to open her mouth and outright lie. That'd get her cell taken away for a month if Ingrid found out.

"Movie and popcorn night," Addilyn told me in a sickeningly sweet tone, playing my game. "I can't stand the scent of woodsmoke. Fires make me nervous."

Absolute fucking bullshit, but Ingrid bought it.

"I'm not a fan of flames either, Addilyn," Dad said with a wink. "We had to evacuate Gideon's childhood home twice because of fires down in California."

Ingrid asked him about it, but I kept my focus on Addilyn, narrowing my eyes to let her know I knew she lied.

She glared back—but I kept my thoughts and the truth to myself since Dad pretty much gave her his blessing to go.

Stalking and sneaking onto Devon's property it would be.

19

Addilyn

"**S**o, talking about needing to get laid and V-cards, tonight would be a good time for it," Jenny said, breathless with excitement.

"I'm only interested in getting my first kiss," I reminded her.

We'd made popcorn and locked ourselves in her room, turned up her TV, and readied to go to Devon's.

"Will Gideon be there? I'd love nothing more than to hand it over to him."

I fought off a scowl while applying another layer of mascara. "You can have him. All he ever does is stare at me, and I'm sick of it."

Jenny let out an exaggerated sigh through her nose while rubbing her gloss-slackened lips together to coat them better. "Sounds like heaven to me."

I snorted, angling my head to check my sparkly

eyeshadow's blend from peach to the perfect shade of browns. "Hardly. Every time I turn around, he's there. Lurking. Up my damn ass."

"I wouldn't mind him up *my* ass."

"Gross." I forced a laugh like I'd have done before getting jealous over the idea of my best friend and stepbrother. I elbowed her, smearing the second coat of lipgloss she applied across her cheek.

"Bitch!" She laughed, grabbing a tissue to clean up the mess I'd caused. "I heard anal is hot as fuck. Hurts, but in a good way."

I rolled my eyes even though warmth burst through me at the thought of being held down and taken how I'd secretly fantasized about—more than once.

"Come on." Jenny tossed the dirtied tissue into the trashcan. "I think that's Devon's brother's car lights out there a little ways down the road. Let's live it up—celebrate your sweet sixteen and the warmer weather. You can finally have your first kiss, and maybe I'll get lucky and your brother will show up and give me what I want."

The image of them together flashed through my mind—and my gut twisted up tight. I eyed my best friend as she reapplied her lipgloss. I did not want Gideon touching her. Kissing her. Whispering naughty stuff to her like he did to me.

But why not? If he went for Jenny, he'd leave me alone. Was I…

I'm not jealous.

Flouncing my hair, I focused on the other thing she'd said. Warmer weather meant the school year's end drew closer, and a whole summer lay ahead of us. May also meant Gideon's eighteenth birthday and him moving back to California once he graduated.

But that truth didn't help ease my slight frown. It left me chilled as I slid beside Jenny onto the backseat of Devon's brother's car.

I'd hated my shadow the previous couple of months, but the thought of losing him didn't sit right either. Somehow, I'd gone from despising him to… relying on him. Trusting. And secretly wanting even though I couldn't have him.

Sixteen, and I ended up with my first red, plastic cup of beer in hand, a buzz making me think I could dance. Jenny and I ground against one another, laughing and shouting to hear each other over the thumping music.

Devon's father and mother had gone away for the weekend for their anniversary, leaving Devon's brother as man of the house, but he took off after dropping me and Jenny at their front door. That left Devon in charge of their basement's bar and liquor bottles lining the back wall. Add in a stereo and a few dozen bored teens, and the house rocked from second floor to basement where Jenny and I danced.

Buzzed bodies. Spilled beer. Laughter and face sucking. Probably fucking in the bedrooms upstairs.

While I wasn't in a rush to give up my virginity like Jenny, I enjoyed the hell out of losing my stalker for the night. The lack of the lurker meant Devon, the kid who'd been madly in love with me since the second grade, got a chance to approach me without being told to fuck off by my so-called brother.

Thoughts of Gideon heated me up rather than Devon weaseling his leg between my thighs while we danced. But my eyesight wavered with my first buzz ever, and all was right in the world. Sweat dampened my back and forehead. Still, I danced on, loving the feel of hands on my waist, the hard chest against mine.

Devon wasn't tall like Gideon. Didn't tower over me or melt my panties, but I tasted freedom for the first time in months, and the giddiness of it—along with my buzz—made me want to throw all caution to the wind.

"Want to go outside and cool off?" Devon half-shouted in my ear, his hot breath sending a shiver down my neck. "Bonfire is pretty much toast, but we can still hang out if you want."

"Yeah!" I hollered back.

Jenny elbowed me as we started away and shot two thumbs up. Giggling, I held tight to Devon's hand, nearly tripping in my haste to keep up with his hurried steps.

"Where we going?" I asked with a laugh as he shoved open the slider leading into their back yard and pulled me after him.

Cool air swept over my heated skin, sending another shiver through me. A few of his buddies stood around the remains of the bonfire a little ways to our right, but rather than head for them, he went straight toward the tree line beyond the yard.

"Thanks for not bringing Gideon along with you tonight."

I snorted, still stumbling after him as he clutched my hand. "Why?"

"So I could finally have a chance to do this."

My body spun, and I found my back against a tree—and Devon's mouth on mine.

First kiss...

Devon moved his lips with ease, soft yet determined, and I wound my arms around his neck, parting my mouth at the stroke of his tongue.

I waited for the fireworks. The consuming lust that would make me want to lay down and spread my legs regardless of his friends cat-calling our way.

Nothing. Not one burst of a spark, no heat between my thighs.

Could a first kiss be any more disappointing?

Thoughts of Gideon and his promised kiss if I'd

wanted it filtered through my mind, making my heart race.

Devon's mouth was just…wrong.

Shivers slid down my spine, waking the fine hairs on my skin as he stroked my tongue—but I recognized the awareness for what it was.

Gideon…

"I'll fucking kill you!" a voice roared, one my spinning head knew.

Devon ripped away from me, and I blinked open my eyes, trying to focus on the swimming scene in front of me.

A flying fist.

A crunch.

Another blur of fists. Curses and blood. Hollering and the wet sound of flesh colliding.

Devon's groan as he sank to the ground registered, his face a mess of red. He'd been beat to shit, I slowly realized—and lay there, unmoving.

I lifted my head, but my eyes took time to make out the hulking beast I blinked into focus. A chest-heaving hunk of gorgeous male with dark wet splotches covering his sweatshirt.

Warmth grew where it shouldn't have.

"What the hell, Gideon?" I slurred, smacking his way but missing his arm.

Devon's friends shouted again, and one started toward us, but Gideon growled at him like a damn bear, pulling him up short.

"He's not allowed to have you." Gideon turned his furious gaze on my face again.

Swaying, I stomped my foot. "I wanted him to!"

"Did you?" Gideon moved in on me faster than I could escape, and my back slammed into the tree again. His face lowered. Hot breath caressed my lips. "Did you really?"

Well, shit.

The arousal missing from Devon's kiss swelled between my thighs, and I gulped, blinking up into wild, animalistic eyes made darker by the night surrounding us.

Time seemed to slow—silence grew heavy, thick with a tension my buzzed brain couldn't make sense of.

Had his violence turned me on? Devon's blood all over Gideon's fists? Or was it simply him being all up in my personal space?

He was like a vortex of energy sucking me into him…

And I stood powerless to withstand his draw.

"*No* one touches you." Gideon grabbed hold of my arm before I could lean into him, and he dragged me up the slight incline toward the front yard, his steps sure and determined while I stumbled to keep up with him.

"Asshole!" someone called after us, bringing clarity once more to my mind.

I hissed and wrenched against Gideon's hold, but

he didn't ease up as we left Devon behind. A quick glance over my shoulder made my head spin, but I was able to focus on the fact his buddies huddled around him. "You hurt him!"

"Yeah? I warned him to keep his hands to himself, didn't I?"

I pulled against Gideon's hold again, but his fingers dug deeper into my forearm. The pain registered—and turned me on.

Sick—I'm so sick.

"It's my body, and he can touch me if I want him to!" I shrieked, smacking at his bloodied hand wrapped around my arm but only out of anger at myself, for getting aroused by his aggression.

Gideon yanked open the door to his Cherokee and tossed me into the passenger seat like I weighed nothing before slamming me inside.

Even new, the interior held the essence of Gideon. Soap and dryer sheets—no rich cologne for the California boy.

He smelled damn delicious, and filling my lungs clear to the brim while he rounded the vehicle tightened my lower belly and made my insides ache for something I'd only read and fantasized about.

Something I couldn't have. Something I told myself I didn't want, even though my body disagreed.

Thoroughly.

Scowling, I pulled my cell from my back pocket

and texted Jenny, letting her know I was heading home.

He climbed in beside me. "Who are you talking to?"

"None of your goddamn business," I snapped, shoving my cell into my pocket. I crossed my arms and stared out the passenger window, hating what his nearness, his protective nature did to my body.

Gideon would take me home, Mother would find out I hadn't been at Jenny's house, and I'd be grounded along with losing my cell for at least a month.

He didn't speak the rest of the ride.

So I didn't either.

20

Gideon

That little shit was lucky I didn't wreck his face more than I had. Sure, his nose had crunched under my fist and I might've broken his jaw, but I'd wanted to do more. Smash in his eye sockets and temple. Fucking ruin him, bury him six feet under for thinking he could put his hands on my princess.

My dick ached from the adrenaline rush, from getting up in her face as that dipshit bled at her feet. Seeing her mouth swollen from his, those lips parted, panting as I crowded in all close had me turned upside down.

Fuck.

I adjusted myself in my jeans, casting a quick glance at the back of her head as she stared out the passenger window like a petulant child.

She'd *wanted* him to touch her? The fuck was

wrong with her? He couldn't be more than five foot nine—if that—with small-ass feet. Probably had a pencil dick too. Semi-rich boy, sheriff's son. *He* was good enough for her...

I blasted the radio, hating the fucking country shit the stations in Anchorage played, but at least I didn't have to talk to the sulking princess the twenty minutes it took me to drive back home. Not that I knew what the fuck to say.

My temper had gotten the best of me, but hadn't I given Devon a warning to not push? He'd been ballsy enough to ignore me. I'd expected him to land at least one punch worth a damn. As it was, his fists missed, easily weaved past me.

Fucking pussy.

Stepping in and breaking them up had pissed her off, but that was what overly protective stepbrothers were supposed to do, right?

What they shouldn't do was get a hard-on whenever she was within three feet. No amount of jerking off rid my mind of her. No matter how raw my dick got or how my wrist ached, I couldn't blow a wad big enough to empty my balls' need for her.

Something had to goddamn give before I made a mistake and put us both in a shit ton of trouble.

The second I parked the car, Addilyn jumped out and attempted to stomp up the driveway with weaving steps, her flouncing hair and swaying hips pulling me in.

She had no fucking clue what she did to me, how unstable our future was because I'd damn near lost my shit on Devon—and the fucking adrenaline demanded I let my blood rage loose on her.

My still-hard dick had me sniffing up her ass the whole way toward the front door.

Sunshine and goddamn peaches.

Fuck it.

I reached out and grabbed the handle before she could and pressed every hard inch of my front along her back, so damn desperate for release, I couldn't think straight. Twining my free hand in her hair, I held on tight.

"Gideon…" She all but gulped my name and lay her cheek against the door, eyelashes fluttering shut.

No headbutt like she'd done the other time I'd gotten too close for her liking.

No cursing, no name calling…

A shudder rippled through her as I sniffed the sweet scent of her, using my grip on her hair to turn her face, my nose tracking behind her ear to the nape of her neck. Her skin sparked maddening lust inside me, dizzying my fucking head better than any joint, evading every cell inside my body and giving me a goddamn high like none other.

"Do you know how hard it is for me to not touch you, princess?" I asked, breathing hot along her ear, imagining how fucking euphoric it would be to stretch her tight pussy with my dick. "Fuck. I can't…" *Shit.* "I can't. If I do—"

Goddamnit!

I gave into the need to grind my aching length against her lower back, my spine tingling and balls tightening as I pulled on her hair hard enough she whimpered—with fucking *need*.

"I-If you do, what?" she whispered, the corner of her lips tempting me to take what she'd given Devon and demolish that memory for life.

She'd been drinking beer, but I didn't doubt her mouth would taste sweet as cherries.

"He'll send me away," I answered rather than finding out for myself.

Another grind of my hips, a harsh tug on her hair, and she gasped, biting on her lower lip.

"Goddamnit, Add—"

The door wrenched open, and she tumbled forward out of my arms—right into Dad's. She jerked away from him as though his touch burned her, and she stumbled up the stairs where safety could be found.

My teeth clenched as Dad watched her go, and I fisted my hands at my sides, still standing on the damn stoop, my heart pounding. Balls aching.

Fuck. He fucking saw. Goddamn surveillance shit he had installed…

One fucking costly mistake, one my mind scrambled to explain—

Dad turned toward me, his face as cold as always when he glanced down over me. Thank fuck my sweatshirt hung low over my belt, somewhat hiding my raging boner. "The hell was that about?" he asked.

"She's upset." I glanced up the stairwell she'd disappeared into, brain still ramped up on finding an excuse, on blowing my load.

"Obviously."

Knowing I had to redirect his focus away from whatever he thought he saw on the doorbell video feed, I went with the truth.

"Some prick was pawing at her at the party she and Jenny snuck out to. Caught him with his tongue down her throat."

Dad's jaw clenched like he felt the same sick jealousy I did. "Who?"

"Devon Bradshaw. Junior—thinks he's big shit."

"Sheriff's son, her little wanna-be boyfriend."

"Yeah," I agreed, even though he hadn't asked a question. The sheriff had become his best friend, so he knew exactly who Devon was.

Lloyd eyed me and my blood-splattered sweatshirt, but I didn't shift or try to hide what I'd done. "I take it you beat his ass for touching her?"

"Bloodied his face up, but his friends were helping him when we left."

My dad dipped his head once and clasped my shoulder. "Good job, son."

All thought fled, and my jaw dropped. An encouraging word *and* an act of affection when fighting before had gotten me tossed into juvie?

"Ingrid is sleeping and doesn't need to know," Dad said, stunning me even further. "We'll keep this to ourselves. I'll talk to Addilyn and tell her the same."

I nodded, dumb and mute.

Dad turned and walked away, leaving me standing there in the open doorway. I stared after him, wondering what the hell had gotten into the man who found negativity in everything I did, who'd been happy to send me away for my anger issues during my earlier teen years.

Addilyn had let me rub all against her backside without hissing like a pissed cat or acting high and mighty like she had a stick up her ass, and Dad all but told me I'd pleased him with the aggression he used to find so distasteful.

I strode into the house—fucking grinning.

21

Addilyn

He'd ruined my first kiss. Broke Devon's face, probably. Then he had to go and wreck my world in so many ways...

But at least Mother's bedroom door had remained closed, her loud snores reaching me through the hall I raced down. Lloyd would ask questions, but I didn't give two shits what Gideon decided to tell him. Lies, truth...it didn't matter. Mother would learn about my sneaking out come morning, and I would face the consequences.

Pulling off my sweatshirt and tossing it into my hamper, I shivered at the memory of muscle against my back. Gideon's arms caging me in. His hardness digging into the top of my ass, the way my scalp still tingled from his harsh hold.

I hated that I couldn't keep from wanting him, how every tiny bit of pain he inflicted turned me on.

Pure…the last thing I was. Heat tingled through my face and chest.

A soft knock sounded on my bedroom door.

"Who is it?" I whisper-hollered, grasping the handle, my pulse once more thrumming.

"It's Lloyd."

Shit. Shit. Shit.

I pulled open the door but stood on the threshold, not inviting him in. Chin lifted, I waited for him to lay down the law and declare punishment for what Jenny and I had done, for the beer he must smell on my breath.

His gaze wandered over my neck for a moment, long enough that I shifted, tipping my head back down. "Your mother is sleeping," he whispered, glancing at their closed bedroom door—as if I couldn't hear her snores. "I'm not going to tell her where you were."

Wait. What?

"I'd figured out what you planned. Devon's dad told me he was throwing a party for you, but I decided to keep it from your mother since every sixteen-year-old girl deserves a chance to get her first kiss if she saved it special for that day." He smiled and tugged on my hair, but without the sting like Gideon had caused.

"N-nothing happened," I lied, hating that my voice shook.

"Well, if any boy tries to touch you without your

consent, you let me know—my son included. And if you're going to be drinking at these sorts of parties, please call me. I'll make sure you have a safe ride home."

I couldn't hold his steady gaze, couldn't understand why he would promise such a thing, so I picked at a thread on the hem of my T-shirt. "Okay."

"Now get yourself in bed. Chances are, your mother's sleeping pills will keep her in bed late. I won't state otherwise if you tell her you arrived home from Jenny's early in the morning for whatever reason you decide upon."

He strode away, his steps taking him toward Mother, toward the woman he'd offered to lie by omission to in order to save my ass from punishment.

How could a nice guy like him have such an asshole for a son?

I quietly shut my door and leaned against it, my mind going back to Gideon and what he'd done.

"Damn jackass," I muttered while I shimmied out of my jeans, thinking I needed a long, hot soak in the tub. Drink a shit ton of water and take a couple of Tylenol. Maybe sneak one of Mother's sleeping pills so I could pass out without having to relive that moment of helplessness, of overwhelming need of having him pressed fully against my backside...

Heated breath ghosting across my nape.

The scrape of his scruffy chin over my skin.

Gideon had nosed beneath my ear like he couldn't fill his lungs deep enough with my scent.

And his hard body holding me against the door kept me upright since the feel of him all over my ass weakened my legs to the point of giving out. Had he put his hands on me, beneath my sweatshirt and sought out the areas no man had ever touched, I would've let him.

What the hell is wrong with me? I turned the lock on my bedroom door, scowling at myself. I hated Gideon—

Sounds of the shower sprang to life in our shared bathroom, stealing my focus as it always did. The door on my side stood cracked open an inch, and I stared, catching a shift of a body inside.

Blue sweatshirt that matched the shade of Gideon's eyes.

Dark jeans that clung to his powerful thighs, the knees ripped out.

Skin.

Good God, skin.

My alcohol-numbed feet moved on their own—I swear on all things holy.

How many times had I lain in bed, listening to Gideon shower? How many times had I imagined what he did in there? Shamefully wondered who he thought of whenever a hint of a groan reached my ears.

Too many.

But I'd never been buzzed enough to give into the fantasy of sneaking a better peek of what I'd only seen once before. Strong hand gripping his hard length. Head tipped back, prominent Adam's apple, lower lip between his teeth, eyes hooded while he stared at me.

I'd fantasized over that memory countless times, and yet I hated the jackass whenever he sauntered by me in tight T-shirts that showed off his upper body as well as those low-slung gray sweats that left nothing to the imagination.

The shower door had steamed over, but I could make out the shadowed image of Gideon beyond. Water from the showerhead poured over him, and rivulets of rushing liquid dripping from his long hair soaked over closed eyes and his scruff-lined jaw, snaking along every dip and valley of muscle beneath.

My mouth dried even as sweat broke over my brow and warmth rushed to wet my core.

The perfect amount of chest hair…a narrow line of it leading down over his abs, straight to the hard dick he held in his hand…

Holy. Shit.

A more delicious sight than I'd remembered. Thighs squeezing involuntarily, I gulped the sudden rush of drool, the noise loud in my ears. His hand paused, freezing me in place.

Caught. Fuck, I'm caught again.

Couldn't. Move.

"Come here, princess," his low voice caused goosebumps to prickle over my bare arms.

I couldn't resist the crackling energy radiating off him.

Powerless once more, my feet—autopilot, I swear—took me forward, my shaking hand silently pushing the bathroom door in. I loathed the fact he opened the shower's glass enclosure, letting out a rush of steam and giving me a full-frontal view to die for.

To salivate over.

Those sweats of his had filled my mind with an image of what lay beneath, but my memory didn't do him justice. Long and thick, his cock jutted toward me, his balls tight up against his groin.

And his hand.

I swallowed hard, mesmerized with how he squeezed the base of his length and pulled upward, around the swollen head and back down all while the rain showerhead trickled water over his hard body.

"You look hungry."

I jerked my focus upward, scowling at the smirk on his lips. "Fuck off, Gideon."

"That's what I was doing until I was so rudely interrupted, but the sight of you in nothing but a tank top and panties? Definitely spanking material."

He started to stroke himself again, but I refused to drop my gaze.

Who the hell was I kidding? He held me captive with those blue eyes, hooded and full of lust, the kind that kicked my hormones into hyperdrive. I understood Jenny wanting to climb him like a tree. I thoroughly understood her wanting to be rid of that V-card.

I ached for it.

Gideon stepped closer, hovering at the shower door's edge. Head tipping back, he peered down at me.

Mere feet away.

I could reach out and touch…

He held the base of his cock and pushed it downward, pointing the tip directly at me. "Want to help?"

Guess the lick along my lower lip hadn't gone unnoticed. "No," I whispered—a compete fucking lie and he knew it.

Caressing one side of his penis with his thumb, Gideon kept it angled toward me. Tempting. Tantalizing. Offering.

Clear liquid welled at the slit, and I realized I stared. Panted. My heart thrummed so hard in my chest I wondered if the alcohol I'd consumed made me hallucinate.

Perhaps I'd passed out and dreamed I'd willingly walked into the bathroom. Watched my stepbrother while he jerked off. Squeezed my thighs over thoughts of having his massive cock worked into me. Because with what he packed, there wouldn't be an easy glide, no matter how wet and willing a woman's body—

"Let me paint your lips, princess. Give you a little taste of what you're hungry for."

"God." I gulped again. Ensnared by his hand moving over his length.

Another stroke of his thumb, and that droplet at the flared head dripped toward the shower floor…

"Two little steps, Addilyn," Gideon enticed me with his low, rasped voice that sounded like my insides felt—shredded and ready to combust. "Get on your knees and let me feed you my dick."

"N-no," I whispered again, staring. Trembling.

"On. Your. Knees." He bit the words out, pointing at the marble in front of him.

Still, I hesitated—couldn't flee and yet couldn't make myself obey either.

"Get on your knees for me, or I'll tell your mother where you were tonight."

Bastard.

I shot him a glare.

His head tilted back further, and he pointed his length right at me. "Knees. Now."

Three shuffled steps I didn't plan on and I did as he commanded, regardless of the way he pissed me off. The cool marble of the floor kissed my knees, and I blinked up at Gideon, into eyes once more wild with want. All thoughts vanished from my head.

I was clueless over what to do.

My body combusted into flames beneath his narrowed gaze.

He'll tell on me if I don't, I reminded myself, explaining away my obedience to a direction I hadn't wanted to take. *Drunk—I'm drunk—*

Slickened heat rubbed over my lower lip, and I gasped.

"Fuck, princess." A muscle jumped in his jaw as he smeared his pre-cum all over my parted lips. "Stick out that sassy tongue and taste me."

I flicked out my tongue.

Salt and musk.

Gideon.

Whimpering, I sank onto my haunches, pulling away from him yet still staring up at the guy I told myself I hated. Someone I wasn't supposed to be attracted to, shouldn't allow to touch me like he did.

I licked at the wetness coating my lips.

Someone who shouldn't taste so damn good.

He grabbed hold of my hair and yanked me forward, my widening eyes slamming shut as he shoved his cock past my parted lips. Thick enough my jaw stretched and long enough I gagged.

"Jesus, fuck." His groan brought wetness to smear inside my panties even as my eyes watered, hazing the vision of him looming over me.

Can't breathe.

Rather than panic, I relaxed into his grip like the girls in those porn videos did, allowing him to use me, my nostrils flaring as he cupped my chin. He backed off enough so I could suck in air. Then shoved in again fully, straight into my throat.

My stomach heaved at the force of my gag reflex, but he held steady, blocking off my stomach's contents, and I swallowed to keep from spewing through my nose.

"Christ," he swore through clenched teeth, his abs contracting, his hiss tingling from my nipples to my clit. "So goddamn hard for you—always."

Can't. Breathe.

My hands found his hard thighs, my fingernails digging in but not enough to break skin. I couldn't make a sound past the thick cock choking me.

I shouldn't like that I knelt before him in a worship position, that arousal continued to grow between my legs at his harsh use of my mouth and the tight hold he had on my hair. Even buzzed, shame filtered through, Mother's words of purity and saving myself for someone I loved making me close my eyes.

"Look at me."

Nostrils flared, desperate for air, I did as told. Hooded and heated with lust, his eyes stared down at me, his chin tilted upward like I was less than him. A worthless hole to get him off.

Rather than dig my fingernails into his skin and draw blood, my lungs attempted a whimper. My core spasmed.

"Princess..."

I didn't pull away as he eased up, allowing me to breathe. I didn't bite down on his thrusting length like Mother had told me to do if a guy ever forced me into something I didn't agree to.

Nope. I leaned forward, allowing him to fuck my face like he owned it—because I wanted him to use me.

"Fuck, yeah. Take it all, princess. Swallow down every drop I've got for you." His fist knotted in my hair. Yanked me forward to meet his thrusting hips, tingling pain rippling over my scalp.

A moan rose from my chest, and I squeezed my thighs together. I liked it, I realized—no, I loved his grunts, his curses, like I'd brought him to *his* knees.

That vortex of energy swirled between us, a connection neither of us could deny.

I held his gaze as he used me and came undone.

Two more thrusts, and he jammed in deep again, an eruption of salty cum shooting into my throat, gagging me.

His deep groans pulsed through my core as I struggled to swallow every thick spurt, and I whimpered, desperate for him to touch me, to give me the same relief shuddering through him.

"Goddamnit." Gideon pulled away and slowly

pressed back in my mouth with a last tremor, an excess of his cum dribbling down my chin as he held my stare. The heat in his eyes faded, the coolness from when I'd first met him taking over his blue orbs. "Thought you were an innocent princess," he said, backing off and letting go of my hair as his cock slid from my tongue, "but you suck dick like a queen."

Warmth shouldn't have curled in my belly at his praise.

"Been watching porn, Addilyn? What do you think Ingrid would say if she learned her sweetheart wasn't as pure as she bragged?"

My breath hitched as heat singed my face, and a prickle of shame crawled over me.

Gideon smirked down at me, his chin once more tilting up. "Look how the mighty princess has fallen—"

My insides ignited, and I *did* dig my fingernails into his thighs until he yelped, hopping back beneath the shower's spray. "The fuck!"

"Go to hell, jackass" I spit—literal remnants of his cum coating my mouth—at him and spun on my heel, stumbling like a drunken idiot to escape the bathroom.

I yanked the door shut behind me, but I could feel Gideon's gaze through the oak. I could taste him on my tongue. The lingering thickness of him still aching my throat.

Insides jumpy with the need to punch something, my eyes welled, and I cursed every bad word I knew. Cursed Gideon, cursed his dad. Most of all, I swore at myself for being such a weak idiot and giving into what Mother had warned me about. Submitting to lust. Soiling my purity. Allowing a man to take advantage of the filth I'd filled my mind with.

I'll blame the alcohol.

I burrowed beneath my blankets and called Jenny, spilling it all, sharing my dirtiest, darkest secret, every second of what had transpired, same as I always did to the one person I could trust. Yet she didn't offer comfort for my tears or my confused emotions, just what sounded a lot like jealousy.

"I honestly don't know why you're so upset, Addy," she grumbled. "I would give every cent in the bank to have a moment like that with him. You're so damn lucky, yet you're bawling like it's the most godawful shit you've ever done."

Because it was. She knew Mother's rules, what I'd been taught since I learned the difference between boys and girls.

But to her, those morals didn't matter. Never had.

"Did you get home okay?" I asked quietly, eyes squeezed shut over the fact I'd been behaving like a selfish bitch—like Mother, only thinking about myself. Of course Jenny wouldn't want to hear about the guy she lusted over taking his need for release from her best friend. "I'm sorry I left without telling you."

"Yeah." She blew a breath out. "Drank too much and didn't get a chance to lose my V-card. Now I'm home safe and sound thanks to Devon's brother."

"You'll find someone who deserves it, Jenny. I know you will—and he'll appreciate the gift you saved for him."

"Uh huh. Gotta go."

"Okay." Hanging up, my stomach soured even more.

I had never felt so damn alone in my life.

22

Gideon

I hadn't lied.

The prim and prissy princess took my dick like a champ, swallowing around my choking girth and making me blow before I'd wanted to. She'd sucked me down without complaint too.

"The fuck did I do?" I grumbled at myself, my forehead resting against my arm along the shower's wall, water beating over my bowed head. "Goddamnit."

Gave into a goddamn bloodlust, the need to release the adrenaline I'd been riding high on since seeing Devon's mouth plastered to hers.

Was she running to tell her mother? Saying I'd taken advantage of her being buzzed? She'd been able to walk good enough—no fucking way she'd been too drunk to know what she did.

Still. I hadn't exactly asked.

"Fuck."

I smashed down on the shower handle, cutting the spray off. Scowling, I grabbed the towel from the vanity and rubbed myself dry, ears straining for pounding on my bedroom door. Dad coming to send my ass south early so he'd be free to take what he wanted, what for a split second while shoving Addilyn against the tree I felt sure she'd gladly give me.

But the fucking timing hadn't been right seeing as how I'd just beaten Devon to a bloody pulp.

No sound came from Addilyn's room, and I closed my eyes while letting out another curse, expecting she'd gone downstairs to tattle like a little brat.

"Jackass," I hissed what she'd called me countless times, owning that shit.

No one came to my room.

The house lay quiet long after, and I stared at my ceiling, naked.

So, she hadn't told on me, but what would the morning bring? The hairs on my neck stirred, a sense of…something ugly ahead.

The shit I did for a girl I shouldn't lust after.

The thought of her tight pussy, those plump lips of hers slick with my pre-cum rather than her usual lip gloss sent a fresh shot of need straight to my groin, leaving me helpless with want.

"Jesus," I whispered harshly, my eyelids slamming

shut as I gave over and grabbed my dick again like the sick fuck I was. Thank fuck a guy couldn't go blind from jerking off.

I imagined her peeking through the bathroom door I'd left open. I could picture her eyeing me through the crack and this time having the guts to come to me without the buzz of alcohol.

Would she climb onto my bed and straddle me with those pale thighs? Shove herself onto my dick and cry over how I much stretched her?

My fingertips tingled with the need to dig into her flesh, yank her down every time she tried to escape the pain my dick caused.

I'd pound the ever loving shit out of her pussy, erase the memory of any other douche who'd snuck a taste that I and her mother hadn't known about.

Fucking sixteen, supposedly untouched.

"Goddamnit." My jaw ached—and my balls let loose, hot spunk spurting up over my abs, my heels digging into the mattress as though I could somehow push deeper into the imaginary princess writhing on my dick.

Gasping for breath, I watched the final dribble of cum leak from my slit, my fingertips wiping it clear and onto the sheet beside me.

"Fuck."

Arm over my face, I allowed myself one last fantasy of Addilyn licking up my abs, loving the taste of me—and whimpering for more.

Rolling to grab my towel off the floor beside my bed didn't sound like a good idea to my beat body, but dried spunk all crusty in my happy trail sounded even worse. Two minutes later, I burrowed face-down on my bed, arms beneath my pillow.

Daylight would bring a showdown of squalling cats, and if those hairs once more rising on my neck were any indication, possible life changing consequences.

23

Addilyn

At Sunday brunch the next day, I sat quietly with my first hangover headache, my focus on my plate while trying and failing to talk away the guilt still eating at my mind.

Mother and Lloyd murmured about their dinner with friends the night before—and then onto business and stuff they needed to button up at the office on Monday. I ignored the two of them, same as I always did—but mostly due to the nausea swirling in my stomach.

Gideon had yet to make an appearance, and I forced myself to eat my dry toast and ignore the jittery flutters in my muscles. Lloyd had winked when I'd told Mother I hadn't slept well and didn't feel so great so I'd come home from Jenny's before she woke.

But what would Gideon do or say? Would he act

as though nothing had happened same as his father did? Be a jackass like usual?

My leg bounced beneath the table, hard.

"Addilyn Jane," Mother snipped, and I glanced up to find her scowling at me.

The leg stilled immediately. "Sorry, ma'am."

Lips pursed, she returned her attention to the supposed love of her life who sat back in his chair rather than leaning in close like he used to do whenever seated beside her. He didn't seem quite as enamored with her after the last few outbursts.

Guess the unlovable woman finally got on his nerves.

The dining room door slid smoothly open without anything more than a whoosh, and I didn't need to look up to know Gideon had arrived. I could feel his presence as if he'd physically brushed against me, the heat and friction of skin on skin pebbling mine from neck to knees.

Jackass.

Scowling over my heating face, I feigned interest in my toast as though starved, the memory of his thickness lodged in my throat choking off my desire to eat—and making me what he always claimed I was.

Shamefully wet.

Shit, if Mother ever learned what her pure daughter had done, the depraved act she'd been enticed into by her stepbrother...

I swallowed down rising bile.

Gideon sat across from me, and I didn't give him the time of day, even though his stare sent pulses through my core regardless of my stomach wanting to upheave.

"Hungry, sis?"

"Don't call me sis," I hissed, shooting daggers at him from my eyes. But I feared my lust for more of what I'd tasted the night before shone in my gaze rather than the shame and anger twisting my gut.

He smirked, those blue eyes knowing. Winked while helping himself to the bowl of scrambled eggs the housekeeper had set on the table.

I tore my focus off the delicious perfection of him and went back to the toast that tasted like cardboard and made my mouth just as dry. The perfect food to settle my belly that refused to calm.

The doorbell rang, pausing the clinking of silverware and murmur of our parents' voices.

Lloyd wiped his lips with his napkin and pushed to stand. "I'll get it, darling," he told Mother.

She beamed up at him, and I rolled my eyes, returning my focus to the crust still in my hand. One more bite, and I could escape her and Gideon.

Murmurs from the foyer. Male, I noted as their footsteps approached.

I glanced up to find Lloyd's brow furrowed as he walked back into the dining room. Two cops followed behind him—one being the sheriff.

"Gideon Destil?" Sheriff Bradshaw rounded the table, intent on my stepbrother.

Oh shit...oh shit... I swung my gaze toward Gideon, my eyes wide—toast lodging in my throat and causing me to swallow hard.

"Yeah?" Gideon replied, gaze jumping from one cop to the other, his back ramrod straight.

"You're under arrest for assault in the first degree against my son."

My heart stuttered. "What?" I gasped.

Gideon simply stared at the cop.

"You have the right to remain silent…" The sheriff's voice faded to a buzz in my ears as he pulled Gideon from his chair and spun him, snapping cuffs around his wrists.

"Lloyd!" Mother said, rising to stand. "What is going on?"

Her husband rounded through my periphery to grasp her hand, murmuring something I didn't hear, but I couldn't bear to tear my attention off Gideon to repeat Mother's question.

He peered at me, his eyes fathomless. Empty of heat and teasing. He didn't listen to the sheriff reading his rights any more than I did as the world closed in on us—in silence.

"Gideon?" I whispered, my eyes welling and causing his image to swim before me.

"Stay away from him, Addilyn," he whispered back, his voice ragged, his steady stare begging me to obey him like I had willingly done the night before. "Stay away from him!"

The other cop jerked Gideon toward the door behind Devon's father, breaking the connection between us.

Mother and Lloyd followed on their heels.

I sat in silence at the large dining room table. Alone and frozen in my seat. My ears buzzing and brain unable to process what had happened.

Handcuffs.

Gideon being read his rights.

My stepbrother, my protector, the jackass I shouldn't want…was getting taken away from me.

"Gideon…" His name tore like a gasped whisper past my lips.

A tremor rippled over me, adrenaline rushing throughout my entire body.

I leaped up and sped through the foyer and out onto the porch, my gaze flitting, searching. Desperately seeking as I pulled up short of fleeing down the front stairs.

The sheriff handed Lloyd a packet of papers in my periphery while the other cop tucked Gideon into the cruiser with its flashing lights atop.

Blue and red. Blinding.

The clang of the car's door hit my ears with a finality that stole my breath away, causing my temples to throb.

Gideon peered at me through the closed window,

his shoulders rounded beneath his black T-shirt. "Stay away from him," he mouthed at me, his eyes pleading, hair tumbling over his brow.

What are you talking about? What's going on? I wanted to shout back while hugging myself tight against the cold creeping up through my center, choking my lungs, and keeping me captive on the porch.

I slumped down onto the top step, rocking myself. My gaze remained locked on Gideon until the cop car pulled away, leaving me with a migraine from hell and a head full of confusion. Tears coursed over my cheeks.

"I want answers, Lloyd!" Mother said while striding past me toward the front door I'd left hanging open. "You need to explain this mess to me!" Her voice echoed in the foyer beyond.

"Come along, sweetheart." Lloyd grasped my elbow and helped me to stand.

"W-why didn't you stop them?" I asked, my lips as numb as my icy heart.

"They had a warrant—and you saw what happened last night."

"It was just a little fight!" I argued, hugging myself tighter as he steadied me on my feet. "Just a couple of young guys acting like...like guys!"

Lloyd held me close, tucking me against his side as we stood on the porch.

I clung to him, sniffling against his chest, trying

to take strength from him like I'd done with Gideon what seemed ages ago. My heart broke all over again, ached for Gideon to be brought back to me. I'd wanted him gone for so long…

I'd been wrong. So terribly wrong.

"The sheriff said Gideon threatened to kill him," he stated quietly, squeezing me tighter.

Gideon had done so dozens of times in school—but he hadn't truly meant it, He'd simply been watching out for me. Thinking he kept me safe.

"You have to help him," I cried, stepping away to peer up into Lloyd's dark eyes. "You have to do something!"

"Oh, I will, sweetheart." He shouldn't have smiled. Shouldn't have had a gleam in his gaze over what had transpired. "I promise, in time." The squeeze of his hand on my hip caused ice to rush through my veins.

Lloyd shouldn't have been happy over his son's arrest, but I swore that was the emotion I read on his face.

A shiver slid down my spine like a droplet of cold water. I pulled away to sprint into the house on wobbly legs.

"Addilyn!" Mother called after me from the parlor door, but I ignored her, stumbling up the stairs badly enough to bash my shin against a tread.

"Let her go, darling," Lloyd murmured to Mother behind me. "Everything is going to be fine."

I didn't believe him. Not one damn bit.

"Addilyn Jane!" Mother's shriek rose from the first floor, and I curled into a ball on my bed.

She knew.

Lloyd must have told her the truth.

She called twice more, but I didn't move.

My bedroom door slammed open, but I couldn't stop my tears in order to sit up and face her like she'd expect me to do.

"You lied to me! I trusted you! Your desire to stay pure...yet you snuck out of Jenny's house?" Her voice rang like a shrill fire alarm, making my eardrums bleed. "How dare you! I taught you better than this, Addilyn. You know the consequences for lying, for getting involved with boys—"

"Darling."

Lloyd had arrived.

"No!" Mother shrieked. "I won't be coddled by you, Lloyd. I won't allow you to side with my daughter over me! She's lied, and she's going to suffer the full consequences this time. None of this *taking it easy* on her bullshit!"

He murmured a few things as I pulled my pillow over my head, but I peeled my eyelids open to watch them from beneath the inch between my mattress and soft feathers atop my head.

Lloyd peered at me from over Mother's shoulder while speaking quietly against her ear, his hands running up and down her arms. Whatever he said to her loosened her rigid stance, and she eventually nodded, turning from the room. Shoulders slumped. Head hanging.

The man must have magic words…or something. The Mother Whisperer. A damn godsend, I realized and chose to ignore the strange reaction I'd seen outside. Perhaps I'd been so caught up in my own shame and grief that I'd misread Lloyd's actions and words. Perhaps he'd simply been trying to soothe me, feign a positive attitude to boost my own spirits rather than *happy* about his son's arrest.

He shut the door behind Mother and crossed the room to sit on the edge of my bed. "Addilyn."

I moved the pillow enough to better see him. "What," I rasped, swiping at the wetness on my cheeks.

Lloyd pushed the pillow completely off my head and smoothed back my hair.

Shivers wracked through me, but not the lustful ones Gideon induced. More tears spilled down my cheeks.

"Shh, sweetheart." He rubbed his hand over my back. "I promise I'm going to make things right. Don't I always?"

"Yes," I whispered. I had to trust him. I didn't have anyone else.

"I have to contact a lawyer, figure out what we need to do to get your Gideon home, okay?"

Lips tight to keep from sobbing, I nodded.

Lloyd leaned down and brushed his mouth over my forehead, his heavy inhale fluttering my hair. "Rest, sweetheart. We can talk more once I know what we're up against."

24

Gideon

I knew the second that cop said, "…against my son," that I was fucked. The sheriff shouldn't have been allowed to be the arresting officer or even present for that matter. Him being the one to handcuff me meant he was above the law.

And I was nothing more than an angry punk from the lower forty-eight who hurt one of their own.

Fucked, I told myself again as he led me across the precinct's parking garage in silence. Someone buzzed us through a metal door, and it clanged shut behind me with a finality that promised freedom was a thing of my past.

Assault in the first degree would probably stick, even though all I'd done was bloody Devon's nose. Prosecutors would convince the jury my fists were dangerous instruments—which they were—and I'd get the maximum penalty.

At least the fucker handed me off in prebooking to a different cop who asked me a few questions about my identity. My information went to records to check for warrants, which I knew would come back clean, thanks to Dad.

After getting patted down, my personal shit bagged and taken from me, I wound up standing on a blue X for my mug shot. I kept my chin up, expression hard, eyes cold as hell—my "fuck you" face even though my gut clenched like a kid locked outside after dark.

Being seventeen, I should have gotten a DJJ risk assessment, but that got nixed. No doubt, they planned to try me as an adult, but I didn't say jack shit, didn't ask questions. I would wait for my lawyer.

I got fingerprinted for the third time in my life, and my one request to obtain a bond got ignored.

So did the phone call legally owed me.

My juvenile ass landed in a hard chair at a steel table—and that goddamn one-way window made me want to squirm. Face passive, I sat in silence.

Waiting.

Knowing what was coming.

I'd been through the drill twice before. *Did you beat up that shithead? Who started it?*

They kept my hands cuffed behind my back like the asshole cops thought I was some threat. Dangerous instruments that they were, probably a good fucking idea.

My gut churned with rage, red lust for blood. Hands fisted, I counted every ticking second. Thinking of Addilyn, the terror, the pain on her face.

That connection I'd felt to her—I'd never even imagined such a feeling. I prayed like fuck she obeyed me—stayed away from him.

Stretching my neck side to side, I considered the consequences for that bastard if she didn't. I would end him. Spill his blood, spit on his lifeless body—

The heavy door squeaked open. At least it wasn't the fucking sheriff who finally came in, a folder in his hand.

"Not saying jack shit until I see my lawyer," I stated and clamped my lips shut. While I didn't have a lawyer, I knew Dad would get me one.

The fucker pulled out the chair across the table from me, the metal base scraping over concrete.

Questions got tossed my way one after the other, but I did exactly as I'd said—didn't speak a goddamn word.

Was I at Devon Bradshaw's house the night before?

Dumb fucker knew I'd been—while leading me to the cruiser outside our home, Devon's dad had taunted about the surveillance system around their house. Caught fucking red handed. Literally.

Had I beaten Devon until he collapsed?

I wanted to roll my eyes. Why the fuck did he even ask? They knew the truth. Staring at the gray, cement wall, I ignored the cop's questions, the words registering but not worthy of my answers.

Had I threatened him—twice—the day before in the school's hallway, stating that if he touched Addilyn I would kill him? Slammed him into lockers various times.

They were definitely going all in, I realized. My insides chilled, but I held still. Unmoving as though unaffected, in a world of my own.

Where the fuck is Dad?

I refused to glance at the window but finally lowered my focus and held the damn cop's gaze with a steady one of my own. No remorse would line my face because given the chance, I would beat the shit out of that prick all over again.

My ass ended up in a holding cell.

No Dad.

No lawyer.

Being seventeen kept me from detainment with the other adults in the county jail, and I got my own little cinder-block box. At least I wasn't locked up with a bunch of dick-hungry pervs wanting a piece of me. Then I *would* have to kill a man.

Come morning, my arraignment would clue me

in on the official charge and how much Ingrid would need to lend Dad to bail me out—if either intended to do so. His lack of an appearance kept my stomach in tight knots all through the night.

Didn't sleep worth a shit, but at least a lawyer arrived in the morning, hired by my dad, thank fuck. I'd half expected him to let me rot so he'd have unhindered access to the princess. Maybe I'd read him wrong.

My insides relaxing the slightest bit, I allowed my shoulders to sag as the lawyer sat down across from me.

"I would recommend a plea bargain, Mr. Destil."

I stared a few seconds, processing. "What?"

The lawyer folded his hands and leaned onto the table, not even bothering to open the briefcase he'd brought along for our meeting. "A plea bargain. They're going to charge you as an adult, and the cards are stacked against you, young man. Plead guilty, and you'll get ten max. Maybe be out in five if you behave yourself."

"The. Fuck." I stared at him, but he held my gaze. "Over a goddamn bloody nose?"

"A broken nose, fractured cheekbone, swelling of the brain—he hasn't woken up yet, Gideon."

Christ, I must have hit him hard as fuck. I let out a steady, shaky exhale even though I didn't feel an ounce of regret. I'd warned the little shit—twice. My knuckles throbbed in memory of wrecking his face, and I had to bite back a fucking grin.

I'd do it all over again.

"They have the entire fight on video."

"Grainy as fuck, I'm sure," I tossed out, grasping at straws.

"Still—the group of young men outside at the time will all name you as the man on that video."

"He was touching my sister without her consent," I stated through clenched teeth. My shoulders once more hitched to my ears as that rage rushed back through me, tensing every muscle in my body.

"Devon's friends will state otherwise."

"They were a good fifty yards away," I hollered, sitting back and fisting my hands again.

"She wasn't fighting him in the video."

"Maybe because he had her pinned against the goddamn tree! Ever think of that?"

"Mr. Destil." The lawyer thinned his lips.

I leaned forward. "She didn't want it," I lied. "Ask her."

I could trust my princess—I promised myself I could. Hadn't she been devastated as they'd hauled my ass away? Hadn't she come running after us, tears streaming down her cheeks? Her face as wrecked as her posture while hugging herself?

She would lie for me. I knew she would if only—

"I need to talk to her," I said through gritted teeth.

"That won't be possible." The lawyer lifted his briefcase and finally seemed to do something other than talk. He slid a paper across the table toward me.

"What's this?"

"Your plea bargain."

"I'm not signing shit." I lifted my chin, staring the bastard down. "We're going to fight these charges, and with Addilyn's help, I'm going to be cleared."

"Fighting the inevitable could very well get you more time."

"Fighting will earn me my freedom," I spat back, rousing every ounce of surety I could into my voice.

My gut, however, wasn't as confident.

We went to my arraignment, and I was formally charged with assault in the first degree as well as two other simple assault charges for those locker slams.

What the fuck ever.

I stood before the judge without a single goddamn family member in attendance behind me. Not sure what that meant, but I still pleaded not guilty.

No bail.

Big fucking surprise there too considering the sheriff standing at attention off to my right, a smug as fuck smirk on his face.

Once led back to my cell, I stared at the dark, dank ceiling, arms crossed overhead.

"My princess will lie for me," I whispered to no one.

She had to—or my life was royally fucked, as would be hers. Dad would have unhindered access to my stepsister if what I had suspected from the first was true.

If my freedom was gone, Addilyn's innocence would be destroyed.

25

Addilyn

I lay curled on my side, silence ringing in my ears. I stared at my bathroom door, my brain fuzzy and nose still stuffy from crying on and off all night.

My eyes ached, but at least the tears had eased up.

We'd gotten word the afternoon before that Gideon would probably be tried as an adult.

Devon lay in a coma, his brain swelled from Gideon's fists.

All because of me.

Letting out a whimpered sigh, I rolled onto my back, rubbing my eyes. If I'd allowed Gideon to kiss me like I'd secretly wanted, the party wouldn't have happened. The fight wouldn't have happened.

Gideon would still be laying in his own bed, probably jerking off thinking about me.

I tilted my head to the side, and without giving it thought, I climbed out of my bed and shuffled into the bathroom. His door sat cracked open like he usually left it, and the truth of his absence on the other side squeezed my chest.

I pushed in his door and breathed in the scent of his soap, the masculinity that was all Gideon.

His bed sat unmade. Worn jeans on the floor beside his bureau. Blue T-shirt laying on the foot of his bed.

Swallowing against the ache in my throat, I moved forward and picked up his shirt. I held the cotton to my nose, filling my lungs with his scent—and my breath caught on a sob.

They say you don't know what you have until it's gone. Whoever *they* are, they had it so damn right.

My tormentor, my temptation, my protector.

Gone.

Even being hauled off in cuffs, he told me to stay away from Devon. Always looking out for me…

Wetness trickled down my cheek as I pulled his shirt over my camisole, the arms too long, the hem falling almost to my knees. Curled up on his bed, I rubbed my face against his pillow while crying yet more tears.

I couldn't handle it. Didn't know how to ease the dull pain radiating outward from my chest or how to stop the tears soaking his pillow.

Why had I lied? Going to Jenny's, sneaking out…

All of this could've been avoided if I'd just stuck to the truth like Mother always said.

Lloyd was a master at calming her. If I'd asked him if I could attend the party, I bet he would have talked her into letting me go.

Shoulda, woulda, coulda.

And now, it's too late.

A hearty sob escaped me, and I buried my face in soft flannel-covered feathers.

Lost in my pity party, the dip of the bed startled me. Mother would have chided rather than touched my hair. I let out a loud sob and threw myself into Lloyd's arms.

He held me like Gideon had, and I could almost imagine Lloyd's arms were my protector's, his strength becoming mine.

"Shh," he murmured, running his fingers through my ratted hair.

I clutched at his sleep shirt, wishing it was Gideon's soap scent sucked into my lungs with every inhale. Still, I was thankful to have someone to offer me comfort.

"What the hell is this?"

Mother's shriek stiffened my body, but Lloyd didn't release his hold on me.

"I'm comforting our daughter," he said quietly, and I kept my eyes clenched shut, thinking like a child that if I couldn't see her, she couldn't see me. "Unless you'd rather offer her your arms?"

No reply. Big surprise.

"Head on downstairs for your coffee, darling," Lloyd said, his soothing tone easing my insides even though the words hadn't been meant for me. "I'll join you in a moment. Promise."

Lloyd always kept his promises—and Mother knew it as well.

He let out a heavy exhale and pushed me to arm's length, his thumbs ridding my cheeks of tears. "Did you sleep, sweetheart?"

"Hardly," I croaked, finally opening my eyes.

Lloyd looked like he hadn't slept much either, the lines around his eyes making him appear older—but no less handsome. Tenderness filled his gaze. "I'll talk to her. Explain that she misunderstood what was happening here, okay?"

I went for an appreciative smile, but my lips wobbled. A nod worked just as well, but another tear fell.

"Addilyn…" Lloyd cupped my cheek in his warm palm, and I leaned into his touch, so damn desperate for comfort.

"I feel…lost without him," I whispered, my voice as broken as my heart. "And I can't figure out why. He's been nothing but a pain in my ass, driving me nuts. Leaving dirty laundry everywhere, wet towels on the bathroom floor…" Sniffing, I wiped my face with Gideon's sleeve covering my arm.

"I'm always here for you," Lloyd said.

"I know," I whispered, trying for another smile while tilting my head up.

He glanced down at my lips and smiled too. "While I can never replace my son, I hope you'll be my friend through this trial ahead of us."

"I would like that."

Grasping my hand, he patted it between the two of his. "I think it would be best if we keep our friendship from your mother. She's…unwell and is already jealous of your youth and beauty."

Considering he married a matured version of myself, I expected he thought me beautiful too. Warmth trickled in, replacing some of the coldness in my chest.

"That's probably a good idea," I said with a small huff of laughter.

"You need anything—anything," he said, his tone low, one hand lifting to cradle my cheek again, "I'm here for you."

I nodded, tears once more wanting to roll over having him on my side.

Lloyd leaned in and kissed my forehead, his lips lingering.

"Definitely don't let Mother see you kissing me like that." Another quiet laugh accompanied my whispered words.

He pulled back, chuckling. "I wouldn't dream of it."

Lloyd and Mother hired a lawyer who promised to call after the arraignment. I'd wanted to go, but Mother refused.

It was bad enough I'd rebelled outright for the first time. She wouldn't have me exposed to a place full of miscreants and bad influences.

Guess she saw Gideon as one, even though he'd only been protecting me. Not that I opened my mouth to correct her. She buzzed from alcohol by the time the lawyer called.

Gideon had chosen to plead not guilty, and he was being tried as an adult for assault in the first degree. While I didn't understand what that meant, it didn't sound good. Mother hovered around Lloyd, not giving me a chance to get him alone to ask.

Finally, the day ended, and Lloyd caught up to me as I started toward the stairs. Mother was already in the parlor—probably pouring herself a drink.

"How are you, my friend?" he asked quietly, keeping his distance since the door to the parlor stood open.

"What's going to happen to Gideon?" I asked rather than trying to explain the ache in my chest and the sourness in my stomach.

Lloyd's lips thinned for a moment, his brow furrowing. "He's definitely facing time in jail."

"Oh God." I swallowed hard.

"If the stupid boy had just pled guilty, he could have gotten a lesser sentence. They have the entire fight on video—he has no chance of winning this case."

"He was just trying to protect me."

Lloyd's brow relaxed. "I know, sweetheart, but Devon's dad said the video is conclusive. You weren't fighting off Devon's advances."

"I wasn't," I agreed. Everyone and their siblings knew Devon and I had promised each other our first kiss.

"It was simply sick, petty jealousy that made Gideon act the way he did. Tell me..." Lloyd studied my face long enough that I shifted on the step, wrapping my arms around myself. "Did he ever...touch you sexually? Make unwanted advances?"

I opened my mouth to deny what he suggested, but Mother's constant instruction to tell the truth rang in my ears. "He never meant me any harm," I went with since I didn't believe it to be a lie.

Lloyd's lips thinned for a moment again, and I glanced down at the hard wood tread beneath my feet. "Addilyn, when this goes to court, if you're called as a witness, you'll need to be honest. Tell the whole truth, you understand that, right?"

"Yes, sir," I whispered, hugging myself tighter.

"As much as I want my son back—" Lloyd let out a heavy exhale "—I have no wish for you to suffer, and lying to keep him from punishment will eat away at your pure heart. Please just do what's right in the eyes of the law, and I'll take his place in your life until his return."

I could promise to speak the truth—but Gideon's father could never replace him in my life, in my heart.

"Can you do me a favor?" he asked quietly when I didn't agree to do what he'd asked.

Nodding, I finally lifted my head.

His eyes filled with the kind of emotion I expected my own father had felt for me before he'd been taken away. "Find happiness again, Addilyn. Focus on you, on your future. You're too young to pine away for a man who wouldn't have been anything but a bad influence on you anyway."

Lloyd had known his son longer than I had so his words didn't surprise me.

Gideon *was* a bad influence—of the worst sort, and yet I longed for him more than anything.

"I-I'll try."

"And one other thing." He glanced at the parlor door and stepped closer, his voice lowering. "You need to keep to yourself until this is over. No talking to friends at school about this—even Jenny. We have to stick together since Sheriff Bradshaw holds the power in his hands. You understand?"

"Yes, sir," I whispered.

"In order to protect Gideon, we need to stick closer than we have been in the past. Don't listen to gossip, don't try to correct anyone's thinking. Trust his lawyer and trust me to help my son."

He would—I knew it. Lloyd had proven himself, and nodding my agreement came easy, even though a shiver trickled down my spine like ice water.

26

Gideon

It only took a damn month for my case to go to court. During those long ass days, I sat in a cell by myself, kept from the general public areas of the county jail except for meals. That meant a few hours worth of body weight workouts every day. A shit ton of reading since I had access to the jail's small library. Even more time to stare at the ceiling and relive every second I could remember of being in my princess's presence.

The peach scent of her filling my lungs while I'd pressed against her back. The feel of her satiny skin beneath my nose. The sight of her sunshine smile warming me through.

The warmth of her mouth wrapped around my dick, those luminous eyes peering up at me with wonder, fear...and fucking lust.

I jerked off daily, most days more often remembering her. Thinking of her. Fantasizing of all the things I should've done while I had the freedom to do so.

Lost—and I feared for a long time.

Maximum of ten years. If I got the full sentence, which my lawyer believed I would, by the time I got out, Addilyn would be done with college, married, and have a couple kids—she was that type.

A faithful wife who wouldn't give a jackass like me the time of day.

I prayed like fuck she wouldn't be wearing Devon Bradshaw's ring.

The fucker woke up two days after my arrest, and the lawyer assured me he would be just fine. At least his family had no plans to sue me or my dad for damages.

All that, I'd learned from my lawyer.

Dad never came to see me. He only answered the one time I'd been allowed a call, and even then, he was short with words and his tone. Abrupt. Disappointed in my actions since Addilyn hadn't even needed the interference.

I'd argued that fact—and the fucker hung up on me.

At least I knew he'd never get to call in that one favor I owed him with me being behind bars. Maybe he'd die of carbon monoxide poisoning himself before I got out and I wouldn't be burdened with him in my life anymore.

A man could hope.

My door buzzed, and I sat up, ready to face the day.

Court.

A final chance to fill my eyes with Addilyn, soak in every inch of her, memorize every glance for the years ahead.

The lawyer's pessimism had definitely worn on me. We'd only spoken a handful of times, but he assured me he would do all he could to help get me free of charges—even though there wasn't much he *could* do. We had no evidence contrary to what the prosecution's witnesses would testify to.

We only had my princess and the story she would tell.

I kept my chin lifted while being handcuffed and led into a parking garage. Tucked into the cruiser that would take me to the court. At least the sheriff didn't tag along.

Sheriff Bradshaw sat in the front row on the opposite side of the courtroom behind the prosecutors. Beside him, Devon's face was still discolored, giving me a sweet sense of satisfaction.

Father sat behind my assigned table, his face bland and hard as stone. No Ingrid—and no Addilyn. I refused to frown or allow my shoulders to slump. Mimicking Dad's expression, I faced forward.

I knew Addilyn would be called in as the prosecution's final witness, but I figured her mother kept her out of sight, out of harm's way until she needed to swear an oath to tell the truth and nothing but the truth, so help her God.

The memory of her eyes peering up at me while on her knees sucking my dick, mascara running… the wonder, the want in her gaze, gave me assurance. She would lie for me.

I tucked my hope into her care as court came to order.

The sitting judge was the same one from my arraignment, a friend of the sheriff's if their welcoming nod to one another was any indication. I noted the exchange, my gut twisting.

Chin lifted, I steadied myself and once more took my seat.

Opening arguments painted me as a bully, a reactionary *adult* with anger issues, my own lawyer's little speech after the prosecution's exactly that—little. Short as fuck without a hint of what he would bring to the table in my defense, same as when I'd questioned him. Like Dad used to do, the guy simply said, "Trust me."

The prosecution team went first, wasting a couple hours bringing in witness after witness to tell the tales of how I'd shoved Devon into lockers, threatened him, all the bullshit teenagers do in high school. Not a goddamn one of them met my gaze while spewing their shit—even if they did speak the truth.

And my lawyer? Didn't cross-examine. What could he ask that would refute their words?

It would all come down to Addilyn.

Recess gave us a break from the monotony, but I twitched to return to the courtroom, my knee bouncing, my stomach tight. I skipped the provided lunch, anxious to finally see my princess, have her words set me free.

We traipsed back in after recess, and Devon took the stand. His words confirmed everything already stated by his friends and even the football's team captain I'd also gotten into it with. Unlike everyone else though, Devon looked at me while answering, his smug smirks and hard gaze so like his father's that I wanted to wreck him again.

Re-break his nose. Knock him the fuck out.

Bathe in his fucking blood and bury him six feet under.

My entire body tensed, hands fisted in my cuffs and jaw clenched. I stared the fucker down, hating his freedom to pursue what belonged to me—what had always been mine and I hadn't been man enough to own.

I became obsessed the first time I had seen her, and not taking what I wanted had landed me in more trouble than claiming her ever would've.

Devon stepped down from the witness stand without being cross-examined by my lawyer with a swagger I wanted to knock off-kilter. My glare stayed on him until he sat.

The cop that had come for me with Sheriff Bradshaw took the stand next—what the fuck for, I had no clue. The prosecuting attorney announced evidence, giving papers to the judge—and handing the same to the cop.

"Can you please tell the jury what you found, Officer Shearer?" he asked.

Records.

My records, the ones supposedly wiped clean. Erased—by Dad.

The entire goddamn jury seemed to lean forward, breath held while listening to the shit from my past.

I turned, and Dad held my gaze with a steady one of his own. Cold.

Un-fucking moved.

Unapologetic.

Three prior arrests as a juvenile—for physically assaulting other assholes who'd pissed me off. Broken nose, dislocated shoulder, and a bruised spleen, whatever the fuck that was.

My jaw fucking ached from clenching it as my stomach rolled. Sweat broke out on my forehead even though chills swept up my spine.

The fucker had turned his back on me, planned to help put me away.

All for free access to the one he had truly moved us to Alaska for.

Addilyn Jane Reed.

My princess.

The only one who could save me.

The prosecution called her in, and the court doors creaked open.

She stepped into the room, her mother on her heels—but I didn't give that cunt a second of my time.

White-blond hair pinned atop Addilyn's head. Wide gaze flitting around the courtroom with every hesitant step up the aisle—landing on me last.

My breath left with a grunt at the fear, the need in her eyes as that connection between us once more slammed into place. Arms aching to hold her, fingers digging into my thighs to keep from reaching for her, I stared as she ripped her focus off me. She faced the seat awaiting her like it was some goddamn electric chair that would zap and claim her life if she spoke one wrong word while her mother settled onto the bench behind me.

Addilyn's hand trembled while reaching to lay it atop the Bible. Her gaze flitted toward me and away again as she swore to speak nothing but the truth.

Tell the truth that's in your heart, princess, I wanted to whisper in her ear, give her all the strength she needed to get through the trial of our lives.

She sat, hands hidden behind the stand but without a doubt primly folded atop the suit pants she wore. The jacket couldn't hide her slouched shoulders, nor the shimmery makeup her pale face and red rimmed eyes.

Addilyn shot one last glance my way, and the questions started.

Addilyn

———————————

I'd vomited the breakfast and lunch I'd forced myself to eat.

My temples throbbed regardless of the Tylenol I'd taken.

Every muscle in my body strained tight beneath my skin, like a rubber band stretched taut and ready to snap.

My breath escaped in pants, and I fought for calm so I wouldn't pass out in front of everyone staring at me.

I allowed myself another eyeful of Gideon sitting in a yellow-gold uniform, hair long and hanging over his furrowed brow. Blue eyes that heated me through regardless of the icy countenance on his face. Lips thinned and tight. Cords in his neck prominent as though he fought to sit still and not rush to spirit me away from the courthouse—from my heartache. My pain.

A sense of emptiness swelled inside my chest even as my heartbeat fluttered.

Longing fueled him. Need—and not just to be near me again, I expected. He needed his freedom and wanted to be by my side, same as I wanted to be by his.

Mother hadn't allowed me to sit in on the trial, and Lloyd hadn't shared much of what had happened during the morning hours. He'd simply given me a quick hug and kiss to the top of my head when Mother wasn't looking.

"Just tell the truth," he had whispered before releasing me.

Mother had glanced between us upon turning, and I couldn't bear the accusation in her eyes. She had to know I wanted nothing to do with her husband. Couldn't she see my devastation over Gideon's arrest? Still, my gaze found the floor and had stayed there until I was admitted to the courtroom.

The feel of a million eyes shivered over my skin, but it had been the energy I recognized that lifted my head, kept my focus shifting over faceless bodies until I'd seen him.

Gideon.

My princess, his eyes seemed to say—

"Would you state your name..."

I tore my gaze off my stepbrother and struggled to focus on the prosecuting attorney. All that talk, those movies of meeting with lawyers to go over questions—they'd never schooled me on what to say once I sat on the witness stand. I was going in blind.

Shakiness settled into my muscles, and I struggled to find my voice when asked my name.

More questions came my way, ones requiring replies that didn't hold any sway over the proceedings. I managed to settle into my seat, unclenching my fingers' tight grip on each other.

"Would you please tell the court about your relationship with Gideon Destil."

Easily done, also easy to be honest about, but I caught sight of Devon beyond the prosecuting attorney standing in front of me.

Shading still lay beneath his eye, but no other evidence of injury marked his face. He smiled his goofy grin, but I couldn't find the energy to return the gesture, no matter how much I wanted to apologize for what had happened to him.

Lloyd had demanded I stay away from him in school, so I had. No chatting with him on social media either. We'd shared our first kiss—and hadn't spoken a word since.

"Miss Reed?"

Blinking, I turned my attention to the frowning man in front of me.

My relationship with Gideon.

Yes.

Clearing my throat, I started from the beginning, telling the court about my stepbrother that I hadn't been thrilled to meet. But he turned out to not be so bad, I assured them, my voice still shaking, my brain and lips stumbling over words.

He took me to and from school every day, watched over me like the big brother I hadn't realized I'd wanted.

The first half hour passed easily enough as the questions pertaining to our relationship allowed me to paint him in a caretaker's role, a loving sibling who always tried to protect me. My insides relaxed, and I wondered if Lloyd had somehow talked the prosecuting attorney into taking it easy on me and to not ask questions I would be forced to answer truthfully that might make Gideon look bad.

"Where were you on the night of March twelfth?"

Since I knew they had the two of us kissing on video, I didn't even consider lying. "Devon Bradshaw's." My face warmed, but I refused to glance at either him or Gideon.

"Had you been drinking?"

Did the red cup I'd been holding while dancing get caught on camera? I glanced at Devon. He nodded, encouraging me to tell the truth—as the sheriff's son, he couldn't get busted for all of us drinking at his place, could he?

"Yes?" I answered, my tone suggesting more a question than truth.

"Were you aware of your surroundings?"

"Yes."

"Do you remember taking a walk outside with Devon?"

"Yes."

"Can you tell us what happened from that point onward?"

Nodding, I laced my fingers together tighter on my lap to keep from wiping my palms down my thighs. Face hot, I focused on my white knuckles and had to spill the story about getting my first kiss. My back against the tree, Devon being gentle.

"You gave your consent."

Not a question, but I nodded—telling the truth.

Devon's attorney admitted evidence at that point, the very video I'd known about but hadn't expected to see.

I sat, staring at the screen, my hands aching from squeezing them atop my lap.

A surprisingly decent video in black and white but with no sound appeared on the TV. A couple who was obviously me and Devon stood along the tree line, kissing, and a body barreled down the side yard seconds later.

I relived the absence of fireworks, the disappointment of a first kiss, and how the moment Gideon ripped Devon off me, my heart leaped in my chest. He attacked Devon like a man possessed, and I blinked, baffled as to why warmth spread through me, tingling between my thighs.

Devon fell to the ground, and I held my breath as I watched Gideon approach me, shove me against the tree by my neck. I gulped, my core clenching over his possessiveness, the memory of his rage, the pain from his grip on my arm that had turned me on.

Sick—I'm so damn sick to be aroused by this.

Gideon's sweatshirt had been splattered by blood from the violence he'd unleashed—all because of protecting me or out of jealousy?

Our gazes clashed across the courtroom, the invisible string of energy between us snapping as our eyes held. Reliving the moment together. My pulse thrummed in my neck, and my nipples hardened to tight points. I swallowed back a whimper as the TV went black in my periphery.

"What, Miss Reed, would you say Mr. Destil's actions looked like?"

Gideon's face remained calm while I felt anything but. "He was trying to protect me," I whispered, our focus still on one another, our hearts and minds seemingly in tune even though physical space lay between us.

"It was no secret you waited for and wanted a sweet sixteen kiss with my client," the attorney stated, his tone hinting at sarcasm and making me feel like a toddler as I tore my focus off Gideon.

"Doesn't every young woman dream of a sweet sixteen?" I went for with a forced smile, hoping to gain the female juror's understanding, a connection they might consider when faced with deciding Gideon's fate.

"So, in what way was the accused protecting you if you consented to Devon Bradshaw's attentions?"

"Well…my stepbrother thought I didn't want the kiss."

"Did the video look like you didn't want it—and had you given him any reason to believe otherwise?"

"Well, I've always dreamed of my sweet sixteen—"

"Yes, Miss Reed, you've already informed the court about your fairytales, but this isn't about you," the prosecutor stated, his voice hard. "This is about a young man attempting to beat another to death."

This isn't about you.

My own voice rang in my ears from the argument I'd had with Mother months earlier, stabbing me like a knife through the heart and stealing my breath.

"Tell the truth, Miss Reed," the attorney said, causing me to blink. "Did he or did he not scream, 'I'll fucking kill you,' before punching Mr. Bradshaw in the face as that video so graphically shows?"

My eyelids slammed shut. *Tell the truth,* one of the few things of value Mother had instilled in me. Lloyd had demanded it—suggested it would set us all free.

"The accused has stalked you since he moved to Alaska," the attorney went on as I fought to find words. "Listened in on your phone conversations. Performed unwanted sexual advances. He pushed you for what he knew wasn't legal in the state of Alaska at the time. Isn't that right?"

The blood drained from my face. "Wh-what?"

"According to Jenny Lind—" the attorney went back to his desk, shuffled some papers until picking one up "—Gideon Destil forced you to your knees the same evening after the fight—"

Mother literally hissed from where she'd sat beside Lloyd after following me into the courtroom.

"He didn't force me," I hastened to correct the man, my stomach clenching tight as my fingers on my lap.

Jenny had spilled my secrets.

She sat behind Devon and his family, her head bowed.

"So, you willingly performed fellatio on the accused?"

Oh God.

I squeezed my eyes shut, swallowing against rising bile as Lloyd shushed my mother who whispered harshly.

The judge smashed his gavel onto his desk. "Quiet in the courtroom!"

His booming voice silenced Mother but not my mind.

What has Jenny done?

"According to Miss Lind's testimony, you walked into the bathroom on Mr. Destil masturbating," the attorney stated once given the okay to return to questioning me, and I cringed. "He asked if you wanted to help him…and you told him no."

I couldn't speak.

"He ordered you to your knees and threatened to tell your mother that you had snuck out to attend the party if you didn't obey his command."

"I-It was consensual," I managed to rasp without vomiting.

"Giving in to a man's lust due to a threat is not consent." The prosecuting attorney paused while I fought to breathe, my ears ringing in the stifling silence hovering over the entire courtroom. "He has attempted to intimidate our client countless times, shoved him into lockers." He continued spewing truth as I cowered in my chair, desperately trying to keep from heaving. "Mr. Destil told Devon Bradshaw on two accounts that if he touched you, he would kill him, and almost a dozen witnesses confirmed that fact earlier this morning."

Throat tight, I couldn't speak.

This isn't about me...

"Do you know all of this to be true, Miss Reed?"

Closing my eyes, I swallowed against the dryness attacking my throat. I wanted to lie, needed Gideon free. Needed him filling space with me, feeling the fine hairs raise on my neck whenever he entered a room.

I longed for him in a way I'd never wanted anything in my life.

I opened my eyes, my gaze snagging on Mother, her lips pinched tight and her gaze full of fire that promised punishment of the worst sort.

Tell the truth, I could hear her thoughts, *or so help me God...*

Glancing to Lloyd beside her didn't offer any comfort. His eyes held a softness Mother's never had, and his small nod encouraged me to do what was right.

The pull to look at Gideon knifed at my chest, but I closed my eyes again, unable to face him.

"Yes," I whispered the truth.

"I have no further questions."

Shoulders slumped, I wanted to curl up on the chair and wither away. Sink into the floor, into darkness I wouldn't have to crawl from to blink at the light. Telling the truth was supposed to set a person's soul free, not tighten their chest to the point they struggled for breath.

I'd done the right thing, and yet the pain in the

back of my throat… I'd betrayed Gideon, the same as Jenny had betrayed my trust.

I should have protected him like he'd protected me…

Unable to look at him or bear seeing his disappointment, his anger, I kept my head lowered, retreating into myself.

I'd never felt more alone, afloat in churning waters with no land, no hope in sight.

Weakness plagued me, and I longed for the strength of Gideon's arms to keep me from drowning.

I feared I would never feel them again.

28

Gideon

"Yes," she whispered.

Fucking yes—she told the goddamn truth like she'd been groomed to do since childhood. Stunned, I stared at her downturned head, heaviness sinking into my bones, my heart shriveling into a husk.

Or had she done so in order to get back at me for the threat I'd tossed out to get her to suck my dick? I wouldn't really have told her mother—Addilyn had just needed some incentive to take what she'd been wanting for months. There was no fucking way I'd misread her desire, but I'd heard horror stories of girls consenting and later saying they hadn't.

She'd dropped to her knees without physical force.

Wasn't that consent?

My fucking lawyer didn't have jack shit to say to

Addilyn, and she wouldn't look at me as she was dismissed from the witness stand. The fuck kind of attorney was he? It was like Dad had uncovered my records and told my lawyer what to do in order to control my future.

A future I knew in that moment I'd be cheated from by at least ten years, if not more.

Dad refused to acknowledge me. I didn't exist to his bitch of a wife, and Addilyn?

I stared after her as she walked out of the courtroom, her spine straight. She didn't glance my way.

A haughty princess who'd been forced to blow a guy she'd been wet for since first meeting him. I didn't fucking doubt it. But I guess I'd gone too far—and the bitch decided to ruin me just like she'd promised all those weeks ago.

I had wanted to give her every piece of my soul—fuck I would have, given the chance—and she chose to close me out. Shut me off.

My disappointment in her faded as heat simmered to life in my gut. She'd fucking betrayed the connection between us, the truth of what we could have been. She'd chosen her mother's way of life. And *Devon*.

My hands fisted, the need to beat the shit out of something swelling inside me until that same blood rage overrode my senses.

Addilyn Reed was nothing more than a selfish cunt, just like her mother. Fucking bitch—and I'd fallen for her and those supposed peaceful moments we'd had between us.

Had she been playing me the whole damn time? So damn desperate for attention since Ingrid didn't give her any beyond negativity?

Manipulative, little bitch.

The door closed behind her, and I shifted my focus toward the sheriff, hanging onto the stifled scream of rage growing in my mind.

He smirked, his arms crossed. Devon mirrored his pose.

Fuck Addilyn and fuck her shitface boyfriend.

I faced forward, not giving two shits about my fate. I didn't bother turning to look at Dad. He'd betrayed me, same as the girl he probably couldn't wait to get his hands on.

Fucking sick bastard.

How long until he took his grooming to completion, threatened Addilyn, and stole her innocence? How long until Ingrid found out and raised enough of a stink that he decided to bury the bitch?

Why the fuck do you even care?

I told myself I didn't. My fuckface of a father could have the high and mighty snob. Sure, I'd gotten her on her knees to swallow a few days' worth of cum, but I hadn't taken her down a rung or two like I'd thought.

The princess reigned supreme, but only the jury would decide for how long.

Cold descended over my mind, settling over the rage twisting my stomach. No longer angry, just...numb.

The jury of my non-peers got together in a separate room, and in less than an hour, they came to a verdict.

Guilty.

Sentenced to ten years.

A handful of people clapped at the news, and when being led out, I didn't turn, didn't give the shits behind me the time of day.

They could all go straight to fucking hell.

In ten years I'd be back—and I wouldn't come asking forgiveness.

I would take my revenge.

29

Addilyn

"**G**uilty," Lloyd told me while pulling me into his arms.

I sobbed, knowing doing what he and Mother had ordered sent Gideon where he didn't belong. I should've lied. Should've stood up for him. That desire to sink into the floor flooded through me again, and I truly hated myself in that moment. Hated that my father had wanted a child. Hated that my mother had gone through the bother of carrying me inside her body for almost ten months.

Hollowness took over my chest where my heart shouldn't beat. I resented my body's disregarded of my emotions and the way it continued to fill my lungs with life-giving oxygen.

"How long?" I asked, my hands clinging to Lloyd's suit coat, even as Mother hissed at him to let 'the whore' go.

"Ten years."

Another sob ripped from me, and Mother grabbed hold of my arm, yanking me away from the man she'd tried to replace my father with, a man she obviously didn't want her impure daughter touching.

"You can't put your hands on her like that in public." Her low tone wouldn't reach those in the courthouse's foyer around us, but her actions had earned us some questioning glances.

I swiped my tears from my cheeks, fighting for calm. Bad enough everyone around us knew what I'd done, what Gideon had done to me...and now they got to see Mother's unfounded jealousy.

"Come along, darling." Lloyd hooked his arm through hers, patting her hand. "Let's go home. We can process later."

Mother whispered harshly in his ear, but he continued to murmur, coddling like always. She eventually quieted, and I followed on their heels, knowing I would get an earful for my whorish ways, how I'd soiled myself for my future husband.

"Addilyn," Jenny called from behind us, but I didn't acknowledge her.

We stepped outside into the spring air, and I wrapped my sweater tighter around me.

"Addilyn!" Jenny hollered again.

My best friend. The one I'd thought I could trust. I found someone to lay the blame of Gideon's sentence on since I couldn't bear shouldering it on my own. Ignoring her came easily, and I climbed into the car and slammed the door as she hurried forward in my periphery.

"Addilyn?" Lloyd questioned, eyeing me in the rear view.

"Just go."

He started the car and left Jenny behind—and Mother didn't breathe a word, simply sat seething, her entire body tight and perfectly poised in the passenger seat.

Jenny tried calling a dozen times over the next few days while I wallowed in clashing emotions. She texted twice as much, and I ignored those attempts to reach out to apologize too.

Everything but guilt with its sharp claws turned into a muted gray color in my mind. Numbness replaced my disappointment and anger toward Jenny, but my shame lingered.

Mother drank which meant she passed out more often than not, ignoring the fact I breathed which was fine by me.

I couldn't drag myself out of bed, refused to go to school, and gagged while trying to eat.

A quiet knock on my door on day three? four? let me know it was Lloyd.

"Yes?" I called from where I lay curled on my bed, reliving the courtroom scene and hating myself for doing as I'd been told.

He stuck his head in, catching my gaze. "Jenny is here."

The numbness inside me dissipated like smoke with a strong breeze. I exhaled a heavy sigh and clung to the rekindling anger.

I wasn't surprised she'd shown up. Jenny was like a bulldog and wouldn't let my silence go.

"Is Mother in the parlor?" I asked.

"No. She's resting in our room."

I pushed up to sit, not giving two shits I still had on sleep shorts and a camisole without a bra. Lloyd glanced down over my body, but I couldn't rouse the energy to cover my chest—or even care he probably saw my nipples.

"Want me to have her wait in the parlor?"

"Would you please? I'll be down in a minute."

I pulled on a blue T-shirt of Gideon's I'd stolen from his hamper weeks earlier. It no longer smelled like his soap, but I still searched for it with my nose anytime I pulled it on, hoping to get a whiff of him.

No such luck.

Throat tight, I shuffled down the stairs on bare feet, my legs weak.

I tried to mentally prepare myself for a showdown with Jenny but couldn't figure out what to say. Heat rose inside me, the kind that wanted to destroy like a flamethrower to dry twigs.

Whatever love I'd had for her before had been

burned to ash by her actions. It was time for me to hurt her heart like she'd done to mine.

Unleash, I told myself. *Unload on her like you did to Mother all those months ago. Let her have it, and don't hold back. She doesn't deserve any less.*

"How could you?" I asked through my teeth rather than break down in tears as I walked in to find Jenny hugging herself by the window.

She spun to face me, her face pale, eyes red. "The sheriff himself questioned me, Addilyn. He's the law in this town! What was I supposed to do?"

"Keep your damn mouth shut to protect me! To protect Gideon!" I threw my arms up in the air and stood just inside the door. There was no way I could get any closer and not want to rip her eyes out. "You betrayed my trust, Jenny. I told you what happened in the strictest of confidence—and then I had to sit through the most horrifically embarrassing moment of my life in a courtroom full of people! Everyone knows Gideon all but forced me to give him a blow job—"

"You didn't have to."

Ignoring the unclean feeling crawling over my skin for giving into him, I clamped my lips shut and glared at her snippy tone. She was going to get pissy with me?

"You could have said no and walked away—but you didn't." Jenny's chin lifted, and the heat in her eyes clued me in to where her anger stemmed from

—same as I'd suspected the night I'd buried beneath my blankets and told her what had happened.

"You're jealous."

She glanced away, and I choked on a laugh.

"You're jealous that he never gave you a second look except for when he was trying to get under my skin. You're jealous that he's always wanted me. Could you be any more petty, more ridiculous, Jenny?"

"You're his stepsister," she whispered harshly, hands landing on her hips as she found the guts to face me. "That makes him sick."

"Two months ago you didn't think so. You encouraged me to climb his body like a tree."

"You could have lost your V-card twice over. Devon *and* Gideon. And me?" She snorted her disgust. "I can't even get a guy to ask me out!"

Ugly, green jealousy. Gut-wrenching in its effects...

"You want Devon too?" I asked, my voice finding quiet as even more disappointment and hurt shredded my insides.

"Ever since second grade when he told you he liked you."

I stared at my ex-best friend, the one person I'd believed would stick through me thick or thin. Our children were supposed to grow up together. Maybe even marry.

But Jenny crossed a line I never would've had I

been in her shoes. Shameful secrets like I'd shared with her should never be uncovered by a friend, no matter the consequences of lying.

Pain jabbed at the back of my throat, and I wrapped my arms around myself as time seemed to slow down. Cold settled into my core.

"I want you to leave," I told her, my voice raspy and sounding dead to my own ears. "And lose my cell number." Trusting karma to deal with her, I turned and walked away with my trembling chin held high.

Horribly, devastatingly alone.

I asked Lloyd to have my cell number changed. Asked the housekeeper to lie about my availability if anyone called the landline.

I stayed home from school, unable to stomach being in hallways filled with people who knew what had happened after Gideon had dragged me away from Devon's house. Darkness hung like a thick, swirling cloud over my head, and every other minute of the day, I wondered what my stepbrother was doing. *How* he was doing.

Did he understand my need to be honest?

Did he hate me for it?

On the tenth day after his sentencing while running through the words I'd spoken while on the

witness stand for at least the hundredth time, I realized with vivid clarity that I had done the same thing
to him that Jenny had done to me. I'd betrayed him,
his trust.

He must hate me.

Not knowing his emotions ate at my stomach
like acid, burning a hole in my gut, but I deserved
the pain. I couldn't keep food down, couldn't sleep.
My sulking made home life ten times worse, sending
Mother into fits of shrieking because she couldn't
'handle me and my whorish bitchiness.'

She obviously didn't consider the fact I was like
her in every way—looks, temperament, and
emotional reactions.

I hated myself. Hated her even more with every
passing day and twice as much after she refused to
let me visit Gideon in jail so like Jenny, I could beg
forgiveness I didn't deserve—and didn't expect to
receive.

Lloyd ended up caught in the middle of our daily
arguments, the only time I could unleash the slew of
shit inside me, and I took solace in his hugs after he
coddled Mother into silence and sent her off to bed.

She headed to the spa for a much-needed afternoon of rest and relaxation on what seemed like day
five-hundred and sixty-seven of my life in hell, and I
breathed easier in my room, attempting to get
caught up on schoolwork.

Lloyd had gone to the school board and principal, asking for help for the remainder of my sophomore year. Considering the situation, they agreed to let me learn remotely, along with weekly meetings with two tutors I'd be stuck with until the end of the school year.

At least they were substitute teachers and not other students.

A soft knock sounded on my door, one I recognized from his daily check-ins.

"You can come in," I called to Lloyd while typing up one last answer for the social studies lesson I'd been assigned.

He moved to stand behind me, his hands on my shoulders like he'd done the day before. His light hold made me feel grounded. Steady. A touch I could trust. "How's it going?" he asked.

"Good." I finished the sentence and hit the submit button. "Just completed my last assignment of the day."

He squeezed gently, kneading at muscles that always went tense after hours in front of the computer, and I melted beneath his hands. "Your mother isn't at a spa."

I straightened and spun my chair to face him, his hands falling away from me. "Where is she?"

"She finally agreed to see a therapist."

Letting out a heavy exhale, I relaxed again and muttered, "Thank God."

"But she's going to the spa afterward. That gives

us a few hours of silence."

So, she *had* finally started to get on his nerves too. I huffed a snort while pulling my hair up, glad for said silence. "Hopefully the therapist can get her on some meds to help her chill."

Lloyd reached out and grasped my wrist, stopping my attempts to tame my long locks into a messy bun. "Keep it down."

I peered up at him, a weird twinge radiating through my belly. The kind that made a kid ask for a nightlight—the same feeling I had when I first met him all those months ago. "Huh?"

"Your hair." He removed my hands from the twisted knot atop my head and ran his fingers through my long hair, bringing it back over my shoulders. My arms sank down, palms on my lap, limp.

"What are you doing?" Tone wary, I peered up at him, wondering at the strange way he looked at my hair…my mouth.

Grasping my chin in his palm, he tilted my head up, his thumb brushing along my lower lip.

My scalp prickled.

"Lloyd." I tried to pull from his hold, but he tightened his fingers along my jaw, keeping me in place.

Chills raced through me, raising the hairs on the nape of my neck.

"Things couldn't have worked out any better. All I'd hoped, all I'd planned…"

I stilled, my pulse jumping as I processed what he said, his presence hovering over me. Dominating. Intimidating.

Dark eyes peered into mine, and I shivered, instinctively shrinking against my chair as far as I could go. "What are you doing?" I whispered again, my voice ragged.

He removed his hand from my chin and stepped away.

Oxygen rushed into my lungs.

"Let's have a little chat." Lloyd settled onto the foot of my bed, patting the mattress beside him.

"I-I'm fine right here."

"Come over here and sit beside me, Addilyn." Lips in a thin line, he gave me the stern look I'd only ever seen on Gideon's face. And his tone? It promised punishment if not obeyed.

The last thing I needed was *two* parents pissed off at me. Swallowing, I forced my suddenly shaky legs to hold me while shuffling to do as told.

I settled on the edge of my mattress, plenty of space between us, hands on my lap.

"I spoke with Gideon earlier today."

Straightening, I honed in on Lloyd, desperate for information since Mother hadn't allowed me to visit or write to Gideon and beg forgiveness. "How is he? What did he say?"

Lloyd studied my face, his brow furrowed. "He blames you for his sentencing."

I sagged, my breath catching as my eyelids slid shut. *I knew it.*

"You're dead to him, Addilyn. He never wants to hear from you. See you."

Swallowing hard, I nodded, my chest hollowing out.

Empty.

Aching.

Lloyd brushed my hair over my shoulder, his knuckles trailing down my arm.

"Don't touch me," I whispered, shying away and wrapping my arms around myself to keep from shivering. I didn't deserve comfort—I deserved the pain Lloyd's words had brought back with force.

"Did you know that I have access to your cell phone?" he asked, his fingers twirling through the ends of my hair. "To all your social media? Your search history?"

I frowned as his words took time to fully register in my brain—and the blood rushed from my face, jacking my heart rate from sluggish with pain into hyperdrive. I stared, my stomach threatening to heave as a slow smirk lifted his lips. My stepfather knew what I used to Google late at night while hiding beneath my covers?

"Our little sweetheart isn't so pure," he whispered when my eyes blinked wide.

I gagged on rising bile and swallowed it down.

His smile returned, and a tremor rippled over

me. "Restraining fantasies, Addilyn? Consensual non-consent? Where have you learned of such things?"

Words escaped me as I stared at the only person I thought I had left on my side. "D-Did you tell Mother?" I choked out.

"No." His gaze flitted over my face to my neck. To my heaving chest. "Not yet."

"You're g-going to." I didn't ask a question because why else would he bring the topic up unless to warn me of the sure outburst and screaming match in my near future?

"I was thinking—" Lloyd slid closer and wrapped his hand fully in my hair, tipping my head back "—I ought to tell her, but perhaps you might have something that's worth my silence."

Gulping, I held his stare, shivering over the look I recognized in his eyes.

Lust.

Want.

Sick desire he shouldn't feel for me.

Oh God...

"You can't do this," I whispered, trying to back away from him even as he grasped my hair tighter in his fist. Shoving against his chest proved ineffective, and I whimpered at the rapid racing of my heart.

His hold on my hair ripped at the roots, and my eyes filled with tears at the sting.

"Ow...p-please, Lloyd." I shoved at his chest

again, the need to flee tensing every muscle in my body. "Let me go."

"I helped save you from the attentions of a boy who would have fucked you, stole your heart, and left you for California in May," he stated quietly, his focus on my mouth. "And while I hate he took a first from you I had every intention of claiming, the rest of your firsts will be mine, just like I've been fantasizing about."

"No!" I clobbered his shoulder with a wild hook, and he grasped my wrist hard enough I gasped.

"Don't fight me, sweetheart." One twist of my arm sent me face first onto my mattress, and he held me down, his hold on my hair crushing my cheek against the comforter. "You're going to take what I give you."

"No!" I screamed, scratching at his hand as he pressed my face into the mattress. "Let me go you s-sick f-fuck!" I screamed harder, flailing—punching and kicking whatever I could reach, my chest threatening to explode with how hard my heart pulsed adrenaline through my system.

His hand disappeared from my hair.

I jerked beneath him—and a smashing blow against my temple rang my ears. Knocked me senseless. I lay like a limp rag, breathing. Blinking at the spinning, liquid-like wall of my bedroom. Pain radiated between my ears as I fought to focus.

Stay awake.

"I'm going to give you the world, sweetheart," Lloyd whispered against my ear, his hand sliding up the inside of my limp leg. "And you're going to let me because we both know what a whore you really are. Your mother won't believe you—" he groped me between the thighs "—so don't bother telling her. And if you do?"

Cool air slid over my core as he ripped my leggings clean off my body.

"I'll make it hurt," he promised with a tone I knew to be truth.

Nightmare, I told myself while trying and failing to make my body move, fight him off as he shoved my thighs wide. *This isn't happening.*

Two months earlier, I'd thought my life sucked, that my reality couldn't get worse.

What I wouldn't have given in that moment to have my pre-sixteen days back when all I had to think about was hating how my body reacted to Gideon.

My protector I'd betrayed had tried to warn me while being hauled off in cuffs. He'd told me to stay away from *him*.

If only I'd known he'd meant his father.

THE END

About the Author

Lynn Burke is an international bestselling and award-winning author. A stay-at-home mom, she's a lover of coffee and vino, and with three spawn and two fur babies underfoot, noise levels dictate the daily switch-over time. In her few quiet 'me' moments, she can be found hunched over her Mac, trying to type as fast as her muse spews hot stories.

You can find more about Lynn at her website: www.authorlynnburke.com

Also By Lynn Burke

Abel's Obsession

Divulging Secrets

Healing Storms

In Between

Reluctant Lumberjack

Resisting his Mate

The Playboy Bachelor

Billion Dollar Love Anthology

Blood Born Series

Bonds of Worship Series

Dark Leopards MC

Darkest Desires Series

Devil's Outlaws MC

Elite Escort Series

Fallen Gliders MC

Forbidden Obsession Duet

Found by Fate Series

Midnight Sun Series

Missing Link Series

Risso Family Series

Sandy Ridge Series

Vicious Vipers MC